THE BLOOMSBURY MURDER

An Augusta Peel Mystery Book 3

EMILY ORGAN

Also by Emily Organ

Augusta Peel Series:
Death in Soho
Murder in the Air
The Bloomsbury Murder

Penny Green Series:
Limelight
The Rookery
The Maid's Secret
The Inventor
Curse of the Poppy
The Bermondsey Poisoner
An Unwelcome Guest
Death at the Workhouse
The Gang of St Bride's
Murder in Ratcliffe
The Egyptian Mystery

Churchill & Pemberley Series:
Tragedy at Piddleton Hotel

Chapter 1

I<small>T WAS</small> dark when Elizabeth Thackeray stepped into Gordon Square. The sound of wind-whipped trees swiftly replaced the noise of Bloomsbury's traffic. As a gust surged through the branches, Elizabeth was reminded of waves crashing onto the shore. Above her, clouds scurried across the full moon.

The path was a pale ribbon ahead of her. Bare rose-bushes and leafless shrubs lay hidden in the darkness, biding their time until spring arrived. Elizabeth liked to sit and sketch here during the summer months, inhaling the sweet scent of sun-warmed flowers, but the winter months were no less pleasurable. She enjoyed the wildness of the square, with the fearsome wind tugging at her breath and the moon sporadically lighting her way like the revolving beam of a lighthouse.

It wasn't yet six o'clock but the weather seemed to be urging Elizabeth home to her comfortable room and a supper of warm soup and bread.

Lights flickered in the windows overlooking the square,

reminding her she wasn't out in the wilderness but in the middle of London. That was why she loved Bloomsbury. Its green squares provided her with solace and respite from the bustle of the city until she was ready to return to it again.

Elizabeth was halfway through the square when she felt a chill at the nape of her neck.

Is there someone close by?

She turned to look behind her but saw only dark foliage and pale-grey grass. Turning back to her route, Elizabeth reluctantly quickened her step. She didn't want to walk any faster – she wanted to savour this place before she found herself back out on the street again – but something was making her hurry. Perhaps it was her overactive imagination. Or perhaps it was something else.

The exit from the square was about twenty yards ahead of her. Elizabeth paid less attention to the wind and the moon as she moved, and instead focused on the gate in the railings.

The moment she felt a hand on her shoulder, her breath left her. Instinctively, she tried to run but she was knocked off balance. Her bag fell from her shoulder and her spectacles slipped.

A shadowy figure loomed to her right.

"Get away!" she cried. She was still stumbling, but hadn't yet fallen to the ground. Another push came and she tumbled onto the grass.

This is my last chance to get away.

Elizabeth had no idea where her strength or impulse came from, but she sprung to her feet just as the figure lunged at her, then ran as fast as she could. Her bag, which contained her precious books and sketchbook, was left behind.

Her legs pounding, she fled to the gate at a pace she had never imagined possible. She had no breath left to scream or shout; all she could do was get herself to safety.

Chapter 2

A TALL, bespectacled man in a grey overcoat and bowler hat was waiting for Augusta when she arrived at her bookshop the following morning.

"It says on your door that you open at nine," he said.

"Yes, that's right."

He checked his watch. "It's a minute past."

"I must be running a minute late. Thank you for being so patient." She rested her birdcage on the ground and pulled a set of keys out of her handbag to unlock the door.

"I might not be so patient next time." He peered at the yellow bird in the cage. "Is that a budgerigar?"

"A canary."

"You bring it with you each day, do you?"

"Not *it*. *He*. He's called Sparky. And yes, I do. He has lots of fun in the shop and the customers seem to like him." Augusta opened the door, picked up the cage and stepped inside.

She flicked on the lights and placed Sparky's cage on the counter while the grey-coated customer browsed the shelves.

Augusta's shop had been open for two weeks. Numerous shelves of second-hand books adorned the walls and a well-arranged display had been positioned in the bow window. A wooden staircase led up to a galleried storey above the shop floor. Out the back, several boxes of books were waiting to be repaired in the workshop before she could put them out for sale. It was a time-consuming business and Augusta had been working late into the evenings in an attempt to keep on top of things.

Her customer appeared to be content for the time being. She took off her coat and popped it onto a shelf beneath the counter, then pulled an envelope out of her handbag.

Augusta had met the postman on the stairs as she was leaving her flat that morning and he had handed her an official-looking letter. She examined her typed name and address on the front. The postmark was from the west end of London, so the letter hadn't travelled far. *Who can it be from?*

"What have you got in the way of Dickens?" asked the customer before she had a chance to find out.

"You can see them over there on shelf, under the letter 'D'."

"I meant ones I haven't read."

How should I know which ones you have and haven't read?

Augusta took a deep breath before replying. She found it a struggle to be polite to customers at times. "The books on that shelf are all the ones I have by Dickens at the moment. Are there any other authors you're interested in?"

"I'll have a look."

Deciding to leave him to it, Augusta opened the envelope and unfolded the letter. It was on headed paper bearing the name of a law firm: Bewick, Palmer and Curran.

. . .

Dear Mrs Peel,

I kindly request your assistance in the case of a missing person. A client of mine and his wife are concerned about the wellbeing of their daughter. They have received no word from her for six months, and they believe her to be residing in London at the present time.

My client requests that I find someone capable of discovering her whereabouts, and I would therefore appreciate any assistance you might be able to render in regard to this matter.

I should be grateful if you would call at my offices at your earliest convenience.

The letter was signed by a solicitor named Thomas Bewick.

"What about Jane Austen?" asked the grey-coated customer.

Augusta endeavoured to shift her mind from the contents of the letter to this latest book request.

"Jane Austen?"

"Yes. Haven't you heard of her?"

"Of course I've heard of her. Which of her novels have you read?"

"None."

In which case, if you look under 'A' on the shelves, you should find copies of *Sense and Sensibility* and *Pride and Prejudice* there."

She glanced down at the letter again. *How did a solicitor get hold of my contact details? And why does he think I might be able to help him?*

"These copies look rather old," commented the customer.

"All the books in this shop are second-hand," Augusta

replied. "I've repaired them as best as I can, but any wear and tear is reflected in the price."

The grey-coated man lifted *Sense and Sensibility* from the shelf and examined it closely.

Augusta would have to visit the lawyer to find out more, but she was reluctant to commit herself to any additional work. She was busy with her shop. In fact, she felt it a little impertinent that a lawyer should write and ask her for assistance in the first place. She had never advertised her investigative services, nor had she ever suggested to anyone that she would be interested in undertaking more detective work. She hoped her friend, Detective Inspector Philip Fisher, hadn't recommended her. *Surely he would have asked my permission first.*

She didn't like the manner in which the solicitor had assumed she would carry out this work, yet his request was rather difficult to ignore. *What if some harm has come to the missing daughter?* Augusta felt instant sympathy for her parents.

"Walter Scott?" asked the customer.

"You didn't like the look of *Sense and Sensibility?*"

"I prefer a bit more adventure when I'm reading."

"Have you checked under the letter 'S' on the shelves?"

"I couldn't find it."

Augusta suppressed a sigh as she pointed to the relevant shelf on the opposite wall. The customer nodded and strolled toward it. Augusta willed him to hurry along so she could start on her repairs in the workshop.

"*Ivanhoe,*" commented the grey-coated man. "I've always wanted to read that."

"It's a good story."

He pulled the book off the shelf and brought it over to the counter. "It's quite a nice bookshop you've got here, isn't it?"

The dour man's compliment surprised her.

"Thank you."

"Opposite the British Museum, too. You must get quite a bit of passing trade."

"I do." She had greatly benefited from her friend Lady Hereford's efforts to negotiate an affordable rent on the building. "You'd like to buy *Ivanhoe*, then?"

"Yes, I would. And once I've finished it, I'll come back and see if you've got any more Dickens in."

"Thank you. I'll see what I can do."

Chapter 3

AUGUSTA DECIDED to close her shop at lunchtime to make a short excursion up to the offices of Bewick, Palmer and Curran, which were located in Cavendish Square, just north of Oxford Street. The building looked as though it had once been a Regency townhouse. The lower storey was clad in white stone, while the upper floors had large sash windows with elegant stone surrounds.

Thomas Bewick's fashionable young secretary showed Augusta up to his office on the first floor. The solicitor was seated behind a large, sleek desk facing tall windows that overlooked Cavendish Square. Heavy-framed pictures and frosted-glass mirrors hung on the walls, and two plum-coloured sofas were facing each other in front of an ornate fireplace.

Thomas rose to his feet and greeted Augusta warmly. He looked to be about fifty-five, with tousled grey hair. His eyes were a sparkling icy blue and he had a handsome square jaw. He wore an impeccably tailored suit, and the blue silk handkerchief in his chest pocket matched his tie perfectly.

He strolled out from behind his desk and gestured for Augusta to sit on one of the plum sofas. "What a prompt response to my letter!" His voice was deep and mellifluous. "You must only have received it this morning." He hitched his trousers up at the knee and took a seat on the sofa opposite her, one arm resting along the back.

"Yes, I did."

He smiled. He wasn't as serious and stuffy as she had expected. Perhaps she had been wrong to assume that all solicitors were a little dull.

"You must be wondering why on earth I wrote to you."

"I am. How did you hear about me?"

"I had dinner with a friend last week and we were discussing the case of Robert Jeffreys, that chap who was murdered on his airship. I was fascinated to hear all about the lady detective who had worked on the case."

"Do I happen to know your friend?"

"I don't think so. He's another boring old lawyer, I'm afraid. But he followed the airship murder case in the newspapers and was rather intrigued to learn about your work."

Augusta deemed it necessary to manage the solicitor's expectations. "The thing is, Mr Bewick, I run a bookshop. I'm not a private detective."

He gave a puzzled frown. "Have I summoned the wrong Mrs Peel? There can't be many Augusta Peels in London."

"I'm sure there aren't. You're not mistaken about that, and I was involved in Mr Jeffreys's case, but I mainly repair books and run a bookshop. I've never advertised myself as a private detective."

Thomas ran his fingers through his grey hair. "Then I must apologise. I was under the impression that searching for missing people was work you'd be happy to undertake."

"I'm sure I would if I were a proper private detective. However, I'm not."

"Oh dear." He leaned forward. "Then I suppose I've wasted your time."

"Not necessarily. Having read your letter, I must say that this missing woman case intrigues me. Who is she?"

"Catherine Frankland-Russell, the eldest daughter of Lord and Lady Frankland-Russell. I'll show you a photograph." He sprung up from his seat to fetch an envelope from his desk. "Here you are," he said, handing it to her.

Augusta pulled the photograph out of the envelope and eyed the attractive young woman with dark, bobbed hair and wide, mournful eyes. The photograph had been taken in a studio, with only her head and shoulders visible. She was glancing over one shoulder at the camera, her face unsmiling. From what Augusta could see of her dress, it was made of diaphanous material with sequins at the shoulder.

"She's twenty-one years old and her parents are extremely worried about her," said Thomas. "They haven't heard anything from her for six months."

"What was her last known address?"

"Cheyne Walk in Chelsea. I called at the place, but the current resident has heard nothing of her." He returned to his sofa and sat down again. "Nobody knows where she is. That is to say, I haven't found anybody who does."

"And her parents are sure she's still in London?"

"They're inclined to think so. I suppose she may have moved away, but they tell me she's fond of the city and can't imagine her going elsewhere. The family used to live in London but recently bought a place in Shropshire. Catherine lived with them there for a while, but soon returned. Then the communication between them waned and they haven't received any answer to their last few letters. They don't even know whether she's on the telephone or not."

"Is there any suggestion that she might be in danger?"

"Not as such, but given the fact that nobody appears to have seen her or heard from her for some time, we can't say for sure. It may be that she's living a perfectly happy, carefree existence here in London, but her parents would like reassurance that she's safe and well, at least."

"Do they want her returned to them?"

"No, just a little peace of mind would be enough for them."

"How close is her relationship with her parents?"

"I've been the Frankland-Russell family's solicitor for some years now, and my understanding is that they have a decent relationship with all their children."

"Are any of their other children in London?"

"No, I don't believe so."

"Do you know when Catherine's last communication with her parents took place?"

"It was at the beginning of the summer. She told them about various parties she had attended and suggested she would visit them before the summer was out. They replied but heard nothing back after that."

Augusta thought of the poor couple at their home in Shropshire, no doubt feeling very worried about the well-being of their daughter.

Thomas slapped his thigh, as if to bring an end to the conversation. "I shan't waste another moment of your time, Mrs Peel. I hadn't realised you weren't a practising private detective, and I fear I've interrupted your day by summoning you here so urgently. I do hope you'll forgive me."

"Have you notified the police?"

"Lord Frankland-Russell was quite adamant that he

didn't want them involved at this stage. There may be a perfectly reasonable explanation for Miss Frankland-Russell's suspected disappearance, and he wouldn't want the police dragged into it if that were the case. If our inquiries prompt any concerns about Catherine's welfare, I shall certainly speak to them. However, Lord Frankland-Russell is keen to obtain the services of a private detective for the time being."

"I suppose that's what you'll do, then."

"Yes, there are plenty about. One need only browse the advertisements in the *Evening News* to see how many are plying their trade these days. The trouble is, a fair few are no good. After all, just about any of us could set ourselves up as private detectives, couldn't we? I was keen to find somebody with a record of success. I chose you because I'd heard such positive things about you, Mrs Peel."

She smiled. "That's nice to hear, Mr Bewick."

He grinned and held her gaze. "I'm so sorry this won't come to anything, but it's been delightful to meet you. Oh, and I've been terribly remiss in not offering you a drink! I do apologise. I suppose you'll want to be going on your way now, though."

Augusta thought again of the anguished parents in Shropshire and the missing woman who could be in grave danger. *How difficult will it be to find her?* Telling herself there was no need to get involved, she picked up her handbag, ready to leave. Mr Bewick would have to find someone else to do the job.

"It may seem out of turn for me to say this, Mrs Peel, but I shall risk saying it anyway. I sense some hesitancy on your part. Is it possible that you might consider helping me after all?" His brow furrowed hopefully.

She sighed. "I've just opened a new shop, Mr Bewick. I don't have a great deal of time at the moment."

"Of course. I spoke out of turn, I do apologise. I realise you have other commitments. But if you were to consider taking on the case..."

"You mentioned before that you had forgotten to offer me a drink, Mr Bewick. Perhaps if I were to accept one from you now, we could discuss the matter a little further and I could make a final decision."

He laughed and gave her another broad grin. "The Frankland-Russell family is offering a handsome payment for this."

"Money would not be my motive. The thought of helping a young woman who may have come to harm might move me to act, however."

"Absolutely! It's a dreadful worry. I'll ask my secretary to fetch you a drink. What would you like? Sherry? Brandy?"

"A cup of tea will be fine, thank you."

Once the secretary had been summoned and the order placed, Augusta and the solicitor discussed the case in greater detail.

"Does Miss Frankland-Russell have any access to money?" she asked.

"She has a moderate trust, which she's entitled to draw from. However, I recently contacted the administrators of the trust and no withdrawals had been made for some time."

"That's rather worrying. Either she has obtained funds from elsewhere or, for reasons too awful to consider, she hasn't been able to make any withdrawals. It seems rather strange that she left the Chelsea address without anybody knowing where she was going. Is there a chance she might have willingly disappeared?"

"I don't see why she would do so willingly, but it's a possibility we must consider, I suppose."

"Have you made any enquiries yourself?"

"Oh yes, lots! But I've made no progress at all, I'm afraid."

"Perhaps you could give me a list of all the people you've already contacted."

"Yes, gladly. The list is over there on my desk – just remind me to give it to you before you leave. Does this mean you might be willing to take on the case after all?"

"I suppose so. My curiosity is piqued and I'm becoming increasingly worried about Miss Frankland-Russell."

"Thank you, Mrs Peel! We really need someone with your expertise to help us. Lord Frankland-Russell will be overjoyed when I tell him."

Chapter 4

"LORD AND LADY FRANKLAND-RUSSELL," mused Lady Hereford, propped up against an abundance of pillows in her hospital bed that evening. She had wavy white hair and wore a pink bed jacket trimmed with pom-poms. A circle of pink rouge had been rubbed onto each cheek.

Augusta was sitting in the chair beside Lady Hereford's bed. A pleasant rose water scent hung in the air.

"Lady Frankland-Russell used to be a Rathbone. She's the third daughter of the Earl of Rathbone," continued Lady Hereford. "I didn't go to the wedding, but my sister did. Rather ostentatious, by all accounts. Her family is from Somerset. I know less about the Frankland-Russells, although I believe they have some Scottish ancestry. They're in Shropshire, you say?"

Augusta nodded, impressed by Lady Hereford's knowledge of Britain's landed gentry.

"Shropshire, hmm... Did they buy Harkup House?"

"I'm afraid I don't know."

"I think it may have been them that bought Harkup

House. It's beginning to ring a bell now. About a year or two ago, it was. I know they had a big place in London at one time. I suppose they wanted something a little smaller."

Augusta imagined that a small house by Lady Hereford's standards would be mansion-sized by an ordinary person's.

"Three daughters, I think they had. And one of them's missing, is that right?"

"Yes, apparently so. She hasn't been in contact with her parents for six months."

"Maybe she simply doesn't want to."

"Yes, I suppose that's a possibility, but it still would be reassuring for the family to know that she's safe."

"Absolutely. I'd be worried if I had a young daughter in London and hadn't heard from her for a while. It's absolutely right that they've asked someone to go looking for her. Why have they asked you, though?"

"It seems I've inadvertently made a name for myself as a private detective."

Lady Hereford laughed. "That's because you've been going about helping that police inspector chap of yours."

"He's just an old friend."

"From the war. Yes, I realise that. And it's no wonder you can never bring yourself to turn him down. He's a very charming man."

Augusta sighed. "That's not the reason why I help him."

"Of course not. I'll say no more, given that he's a married man."

"Detective Inspector Fisher has nothing to do with this case."

"I can quite understand the family's desire not to involve the police. After all, there may be no cause for alarm at all, and our officers are ever so busy these days. How do you intend to go about solving this case?"

"I need to find out whether there's anyone in London who knows her and would be willing to speak to me. Perhaps her parents have friends the lawyer hasn't asked yet. I'm desperate to find out any snippet of information at the moment."

"Yes, I imagine you would be. Now, let me think... Where's that nurse got to with our tea?"

"Perhaps she had to see to something else."

"I suppose there are people here with greater needs than a simple cup of tea, but it does help patients get better, doesn't it?"

"I'm sure it does." Augusta still wasn't sure what Lady Hereford's ailment might be, but as the old lady had never volunteered the information, she felt it rude to ask.

"Anyway," Lady Hereford continued, "let me think who else might know the Frankland-Russell family. I seem to recall that a marriage was once discussed with the Farrell family."

"Who are they?"

"One of these families with ideas far above their status. Mr Farrell made a good deal of money before the war and likes to pretend he's a member of the landed gentry. He has a son named Hugh who lives in London. Perhaps Miss Frankland-Russell decided to look him up."

"It's possible, I suppose. Do you happen to know where Mr Farrell lives?" Augusta couldn't recall seeing his name among Mr Bewick's list of contacts.

"I'm not entirely sure, but he'll be listed in *Boyle's*."

"*Boyle's?*"

"Yes, *Boyle's Court and Country Guide*."

"A book with all the most important people listed in it?"

"That's right. Hugh Farrell should be in there." The old lady wagged a long finger at her visitor. "But don't go alone."

"Why not?"

"He's a bit of a funny one."

"In what sense?"

"Take someone with you."

"Such as?"

"Anybody. I'd come with you myself if I weren't stuck in this bed."

"I really wouldn't know who to ask. Mrs Whitaker, the tailor's wife?"

"I don't think she'd be much help. Besides, you wouldn't get a word in edgeways. That reminds me, how's my little Sparky?"

"He's doing very well."

The old lady beamed. "Wonderful. Does he like helping you in your shop?"

"I think so. He's been singing to the customers."

"How lovely. It's a shame he can't be more help to you than that, though. You've an awful lot of work to be getting on with, Augusta. You could always opt for the quiet life and get married instead, you know."

Chapter 5

AUGUSTA CONSULTED a copy of *Boyle's Court and Country Guide* at Holborn Library the following morning and discovered that Hugh Farrell lived on Clifford Street in Mayfair.

A short while later, she called at the smart, four-storey townhouse.

A maid answered and confirmed that Mr Farrell was at home. Augusta mentioned Lady Hereford's name and waited in the hallway while the maid went to ask whether he was accepting visitors.

It seemed he was, and Augusta was soon shown into a spacious drawing room with heavy antique furniture, red wallpaper and an oriental carpet in rich tones.

Augusta estimated that Hugh was about fifty years of age. There was something a little old-fashioned about the style of his suit and waistcoat, as if he were still hankering after pre-war Edwardian times.

"Mrs Augusta Peel," he said with a smile. He had chubby cheeks and a pointed beard. His eyes were small, and he narrowed them as he looked her up and down. "A friend of Lady Hereford's, I hear."

Augusta nodded. She was fortunate to be able to use the name of her well-known friend.

Hugh gestured for her to sit on a chaise longue beside a small harpsichord, while he relaxed himself into an easy chair by the fire.

"Daisy will bring us some tea in just a moment. Now, to what do I owe the pleasure of a visit from such an attractive young lady?"

Augusta felt a sour taste in her mouth as he ran his eyes over her again. She decided to keep the conversation as short as possible. "I'm looking for a young lady who's gone missing."

"Missing? How awful!" There was something insincere about the manner in which his eyes grew wide and his mouth hung open. "You think I might have seen her, do you? Who is she?"

"Her name is Miss Catherine Frankland-Russell."

"Not dear Catherine? How dreadful! How long has she been missing?"

"Her parents haven't heard from her for about six months, and they're growing quite concerned."

He nodded earnestly. "I can imagine. They're very good friends of mine. It must be truly awful for them."

"Have they approached you about this?"

He stroked his pointed beard. "Not yet, no… But then I haven't seen Lord Frankland-Russell for almost a year. What can I do to help?"

"You can help me find his daughter."

"Absolutely, absolutely."

"Have you heard from her at all?"

"No, no. I haven't seen Catherine for some time."

"Do you know any of her friends?"

He pushed out his lower lip and shook his head. "Not really. All I can recall is one of her little friends from when she was about twelve."

"I presume the friend isn't quite so little now."

Hugh laughed enthusiastically at this. "No, she'd be a grown woman just like Catherine by now. Elizabeth Thackeray was her name; daughter of Sir Peter Thackeray, another good friend of mine. I must look them up again."

"Do you think there's any chance Miss Frankland-Russell might still be friends with Elizabeth Thackeray?"

"The not-so-little Elizabeth Thackeray? I suppose there's a possibility. I did receive a letter from Mr and Mrs Thackeray quite recently containing news of their family. I'm sure they mentioned what their children were up to these days."

He picked up a little bell by the side of his chair and rang it.

A moment later, a maid entered the room.

"Bessy, can you have a look on my writing desk for any recent correspondence from Mr and Mrs Thackeray?"

Bessy nodded and left the room. As she did so, another maid entered with a tea tray.

"Marvellous." Hugh smacked his lips. "Here's the tea."

Augusta wondered whether Mr Farrell lived in this house with other family members or had numerous servants to wait on him alone. There had been no mention of a wife or children.

"Tell me about yourself, Mrs Peel." He sat back in his chair and steepled his fingers.

This wasn't the direction Augusta had wanted the conversation to take. "There isn't much to tell."

He smirked. "Oh, come now. There must be."

"I run a bookshop."

"You run a bookshop? How fascinating. Whereabouts?"

She felt reluctant to tell him exactly where in case he decided to pay her a visit.

"In Bloomsbury."

"Bloomsbury, where else? The perfect place for a bookshop, I'd say. What sort of books do you sell?"

"Second-hand books I have repaired myself."

"Second-hand books, eh? I've heard that some fetch a fair price these days. Do you stock any valuable volumes?"

"No, not particularly."

"How is it that a lady who runs a bookshop finds herself looking for Catherine Frankland-Russell?"

"The Frankland-Russells' family lawyer asked me to help them find her."

"Why you?"

"I've been wondering the same thing myself."

Bessy returned with the letter Hugh had requested and Augusta felt relieved that she wouldn't have to give any further explanation.

"Thank you, Bessy." He pulled the letter out of its envelope and read it in silence.

Augusta stared at the teapot, wondering when the tea was to be poured. *Would it be rude to pour it out myself?*

Hugh tucked the letter back inside its envelope and rested it on the table next to his chair. Augusta had hoped he would tell her what it said. He seemed to enjoy detaining her and drawing the conversation out. She didn't like it one bit.

"Is there any news of Elizabeth Thackeray in the letter?" she asked as patiently as possible.

"Oh, yes. It describes what each of the children is doing."

"What is Miss Thackeray doing these days?"

"Well, that all rather depends." He steepled his fingers again and smiled.

Once again, Augusta sensed he was deliberately withholding the information she wanted for his own entertainment. His eyes ran over her form once again and she felt her stomach turn.

"Depends on *what?*" she snapped.

"Is there anything you can give me in return?"

"Only the knowledge that you may be helping me search for the missing daughter of a friend."

"There is that, I suppose. I do like to consider myself an honourable man."

"Good. Then perhaps you could tell me whether the letter gives us any clue as to Elizabeth's whereabouts."

"She's doing rather well for herself, apparently. Clearly a modern young woman. She's studying at the Slade School of Fine Art."

Augusta was pleased to hear this. She happened to know that the art school was part of University College London and just happened to be located in Bloomsbury. She smiled, realising she wouldn't have to go far to find Miss Thackeray. She just hoped the girl knew something of note with regard to Miss Frankland-Russell.

"That's excellent. Thank you very much, Mr Farrell. You've been extremely helpful."

"You speak as if you're ready to leave, Mrs Peel. You haven't had any tea yet."

"At the risk of sounding a little rude, Mr Farrell, I've been waiting rather a while for it to be poured out."

"I do apologise. Let's see to that at once." He rang his little bell again and the maid reappeared.

"Could you pour out our tea, Daisy?"

Augusta didn't want to have tea with Hugh Farrell; she wanted to leave immediately. Daisy's presence brought her a little comfort, but she dreaded being left alone with him. *What was it Lady Hereford said about him? Am I a fool for ignoring her advice?*

Daisy handed Augusta a cup of tea and poured another for her employer before leaving the room again. Augusta was determined to drink hers as quickly as possible and leave.

"Would you like some cake?" he asked.

"No, thank you. Although it does look very nice."

"Yes, it's rather delicious. I have a very good cook." He sipped his tea. "What does *Mr* Peel do?"

Augusta deemed it wise to invent a husband for herself. "He's a supervisor at a printing works in Clerkenwell."

"A supervisor? Not long until he becomes a director, in that case?"

"That would be nice."

"What does he think of his wife owning a bookshop? Is he incapable of giving Mrs Peel the life of comfort she deserves?"

"I don't run my bookshop out of necessity, Mr Farrell. I do so because I enjoy it."

"Oh yes, of course. As is always the way with modern women. It seems many enjoy going into the workplace these days, and some are determined to be quite independent."

"Some women have no choice but to be independent. So many men were lost during the war."

Hugh assumed an air of false concern again and gave a slow nod. "Quite, quite. Awful that so many young men lost their lives, and rather difficult for the ladies, too. Although I suppose for a chap like me it means there are more ladies to go around now!"

He laughed, but Augusta found it impossible to share the joke. She drained her cup, desperate to leave.

"Must you be off in such a hurry, Mrs Peel? We're only just starting to get to know each other."

"With all due respect, Mr Farrell, I didn't visit you today because I wanted to get to know you. I merely wished to ask whether you could help me with my investigation into the whereabouts of Miss Frankland-Russell."

He frowned. "That's all you've come for, is it? You were just after some information from me, and now that you have it you're ready to leave."

"I asked you for your help, Mr Farrell, and you kindly provided it. I'm very grateful for that."

"And so you should be. You called on me without giving any notice whatsoever and found me most hospitable. I didn't have to comply, you know."

"I realise that, and I'm very glad of it."

The mood was growing increasingly uncomfortable. At the beginning there had been something lascivious about his gaze, but now it was tinged with anger.

At the risk of appearing impolite, Augusta picked up her handbag, stood and made her way over to the door. "Thank you once again, Mr Farrell."

He jumped to his feet. Augusta didn't like the swiftness of his movement.

"That's it, is it?"

"I'm not sure I quite understand what it is you want from me, Mr Farrell."

"Just a little more of your company, Mrs Peel." He stepped toward her.

She noted that the door was close by, and that he wasn't yet blocking it.

"Surely that's not too much to ask," he added quietly.

"I'm beginning to find your conduct inappropriate, Mr Farrell. I'm a married woman."

"Do you think I care about that?"

Hugh stepped forward and grabbed her wrist, his eyes fixed on hers. "Come now," he said quietly. "Stay a little longer. There's more I can tell you."

Augusta tried to twist her arm away, but he held fast to her wrist.

"If you don't let go of me, I shall cry out," she threatened.

"And what difference will that make?"

"Your staff will hear."

"They are under strict instructions not to interrupt me when I have company, no matter what they hear."

"Let go of my arm, please."

"Only if you agree to keep me company for a while longer. There's a pot of tea for us to finish yet. Or would you prefer something a little stronger?"

"I don't want anything else to drink."

Augusta wished she had heeded Lady Hereford's warning. This was clearly a habit of his. He was stronger than her, and taller, too.

If the staff wouldn't come if I were to call out, how will I ever get away from him? Putting up a fight would be futile. He could easily overpower me.

"All right. I'll have another cup of tea."

Hugh's grip relaxed, but he held on to Augusta's arm as he guided her back to the chaise longue she had been sitting on. This time he sat down next to her. He smelled of stale perspiration.

"That's more like it," he said.

"I'd feel more comfortable if you were to sit opposite me."

"Oh, but I'm much more comfortable here, Mrs Peel."

Augusta's entire body was tensed, but she said nothing.

He leaned forward and poured out another cup of tea

for them both. Steam rose from their cups. Then he sat back, his knee resting against hers.

How am I going to get out of here?

"Now, where were we? Oh, that's right. You were telling me all about yourself."

"There's really nothing more to say about me."

"Is that so?" Hugh picked up his cup of tea. "Maybe there's no need for further conversation, then. What do you think?" He raised an eyebrow and smiled.

I have to get out of here. If I stay a moment longer I'll find myself in a situation that's impossible to escape from.

In one swift movement, Augusta grabbed his saucer and tipped the hot cup of tea into his lap.

He roared in pain and anger as Augusta jumped up from her seat and dashed out of the door.

Chapter 6

"It's only a piece of apple, Sparky. It's not going to bite you."

The canary regarded her cautiously from his perch on the back of a dining chair.

She held out the morsel of food in her palm. "You like apple. It's your favourite."

This appeared to convince him. He fluttered onto her hand and helped himself to the fruit.

A knock at the door startled them both. Sparky flew up to his usual sanctuary on the curtain rail.

"Who could that be at this hour?" Augusta muttered to herself.

Peering through the peephole in her door, she saw a familiar figure in a trench coat and smart suit. He had already removed his hat. The man had dark, greying hair and narrow, wide-set eyes.

Detective Inspector Philip Fisher greeted her with a warm smile when she opened the door.

"Augusta! It's been a while, hasn't it?"

"It certainly has. come in." She felt relieved to see a friendly face after her ordeal with Hugh Farrell.

Philip stepped inside the room, leaning on his walking stick as he moved, then made himself comfortable on her settee.

"I received a telephone call from Lady Hereford," he announced.

"Really? Why?!" Augusta was surprised by this unforeseen development. *What's Lady Hereford doing contacting Philip?*

"She told me about the unusual task you've been given."

"She telephoned to tell you about that?"

"Yes, and it sounds rather interesting. I do hope Catherine Frankland-Russell can be found safe and well. Her disappearance is certainly a cause for concern."

"Yes. I hope we can track her down. I still don't understand why Lady Hereford telephoned you about it, though."

"She asked me to accompany you to speak to a gentleman she told you about. Mr Farrell, I think his name was. She said he was a friend of the Frankland-Russell family but she felt you shouldn't go to visit him alone."

"She did warn me about him."

"You can't be too careful with some chaps. He sounds like a bit of a funny one. Do let me know when you'd like to visit him."

Augusta felt a pang of shame for taking such a risk. "I already have," she reluctantly admitted.

"Oh! That was rather hasty. How did it go?"

"He gave me the name of a friend of Miss Frankland-Russell's."

"I see. Then my journey here has been rather a waste."

"A *waste*?"

"Not quite a waste." He smiled. "I'm sorry. That

sounded rather rude, didn't it? It's good to see you again, Augusta."

"Would a glass of brandy make your visit more worthwhile?"

"A brandy would be lovely, thank you."

Augusta fetched the decanter and poured out two glasses.

"Where's Sparky?" asked Philip, noticing the empty cage.

"Up on the curtain rail above your head."

He looked up and chuckled. "So he is. It must almost be his bedtime."

"Yes, it is. I was just giving him his supper when he was startled by someone knocking at the door."

"Oh dear. I'm sorry to have interrupted his routine. I have a habit of doing that with my son, too. He's often settled and ready for bed, and then I get home from work and make him all over-excited again. It annoys my wife terribly."

Augusta handed him his drink and sat down.

"There was no need for Lady Hereford to have worried about that Farrell chap, then?" he asked.

"There was *every* reason to worry about him. I found him revolting and lecherous."

Philip's face fell. "Oh, goodness. I hope he didn't hurt you. If that man laid a finger on you—"

"It was nothing I couldn't withstand. But he did end up with a hot cup of tea in his lap."

"Oh dear! I'd laugh if the matter wasn't so serious. I wish I'd spoken to you sooner, Augusta. You shouldn't have had to endure that. I shall look him up in the files when I'm back at the Yard tomorrow and see if there's any opportunity to give him a difficult time about something."

"That would be lovely."

Philip shook his head. "Lady Hereford shouldn't really have given you his name."

"She clearly had second thoughts, and that's why she telephoned you."

"I don't suppose she was expecting you to be so hasty about visiting him. Are you sure you're all right?"

"Yes, I'm fine. The worst he did was grab my wrist and then sit rather close to me on the chaise longue."

"At least you managed to get some information out of him. That was all you were after, wasn't it?"

"Yes. The young lady he mentioned is called Elizabeth Thackeray. Apparently, she studies at the Slade School of Fine Art and was a friend of Miss Frankland-Russell's when they were young. There's no guarantee that she knows where she is now, of course, but that's all I have to go on."

"I'm surprised the Frankland-Russells haven't contacted the police yet, given that there has been no word from her for six months. I'd want answers if she were my daughter. Though perhaps she's done this sort of disappearing act before." He took a sip of his drink. "You must let me know how you get on, Augusta. I may be able to help. Though I must say, I'm surprised you agreed to take on the work. I thought you were too busy with your new shop."

"I am! I tried to say no, but there's something about a young woman going missing that I found difficult to ignore. I think I shall have to advertise for some help in the shop. I need someone who can run things while I'm engaged with this task. The solicitor told me there will be some sort of payment, so perhaps I could put the money toward employing someone."

"That makes a lot of sense." Philip sat back and smiled

at her. "I wonder what you really are, Augusta. Are you a bookshop owner or a private detective?"

"A bookshop owner. I'm certainly not a private detective!" She took a gulp of brandy. "Although for some reason, these mysteries seem to have a habit of finding me."

Chapter 7

"This letter for Lord Frankland-Russell is ready for your signature, sir," said Thomas Bewick's secretary, sliding the paper across the desk to him.

"Thank you, Miss Watkins."

Thomas began to read through the letter as she left the room. He wondered how Augusta Peel was faring in her search for Miss Frankland-Russell. She hadn't been given much information to go on.

Is she really as good at solving mysteries as I've heard?

It had only been two days since she had visited, so he couldn't expect her to have made much progress yet, but he felt impatient all the same.

The letter was to inform Lord Frankland-Russell and his wife that the firm had retained the services of a private lady detective to carry out the search for their daughter. He couldn't help feeling pleased with his choice.

Surely a lady detective will find it easier to track down a young woman. Mrs Peel would understand the mind of a young woman better than he ever could. And she was genteel, so anyone she spoke to would consider her less threatening and more approachable than a police officer or male detective. She was the sort of woman who would easily be able to obtain useful information from others.

He was interrupted by Miss Watkins once again.

"My apologies, sir, but there's a lady here to see you. She says she hopes you're not too busy to meet with her."

Thomas consulted his diary. Although he preferred to see clients by appointment, he wasn't averse to seeing people who called in speculatively from time to time.

"I have about ten minutes before my next appointment. Would you mind making that clear to her before you show her in, Miss Watkins? What's her name?"

"Of course, sir. It's Mrs Ellen Mitchell."

Mrs Mitchell was a handsome woman in her mid-thirties. She had fair, jaw-length hair, and her burgundy jacket and skirt were trimmed with silk ribbon. Thomas determined from her appearance that she would most likely be able to afford his fees.

She appeared fidgety and nervous as she seated herself in the chair opposite him. Thomas smiled and did his best to put her at ease.

"What can I help you with, Mrs Mitchell?"

She looked down at her hands. "I've been considering something for a while, and… Well, I hope you don't mind me calling on you like this. One of your cards was dropped through my door and I noticed that there was something in particular you might be able to assist me with…"

"What is it, Mrs Mitchell?"

"I'm… I'm having to summon quite a bit of courage to ask you about this. I… Well, I should like to obtain a divorce."

Thomas relaxed back into his chair and gave her a

reassuring nod to let her know that this wouldn't be a problem at all. She looked visibly relieved.

"I must commend you on your bravery, Mrs Mitchell. I do hope the proverbial weight has lifted from your shoulders a little now that you've had the courage to approach me."

Ellen sniffed and gave a weak smile, her green eyes moist. "Actually, it has. I've been worrying about it for such a long time. Several months, in fact. I've deliberated over it and doubted myself..."

"Of course you have. It's a very difficult decision to arrive at. But rest assured, Mrs Mitchell. I have many clients who have made the same decision and have gone on to lead happy, enjoyable lives after such an event. Although no woman would wish to become a divorcee, these decisions must sometimes be made as a matter of practicality."

"Yes. And it absolutely *is* a matter of practicality."

"Please be encouraged that you've made the right decision by visiting me today, Mrs Mitchell. I conduct business on behalf of a good number of respectable families. Before we discuss your case any further, however, I should like to ensure that you are happy with my fee structure."

He pushed a card across the desk toward her, which set out his basic costs. "I know many lawyers prefer not to discuss fees upfront, but I like to ensure that my clients are fully aware of their financial commitments. I enjoy strong relationships with all my clients, and I believe honesty is crucial from the outset. So I shall ask you to confirm that you are happy with my fees now. If so, we can proceed."

Ellen looked down at the card in front of her, bit the side of her lip, then nodded.

"Is that a yes, Mrs Mitchell?"

"Yes, I'm happy to proceed. Money isn't an enormous

concern of mine, and I'd be very grateful if this matter could be dealt with as quickly as possible."

"Absolutely. Let's see what we can do, shall we?" Thomas whisked the fee card away and readied himself with pen and paper. "Perhaps you can begin by giving me a few details about yourself and your husband."

"My name is Mrs Ellen Mitchell and I own a chain of ladies' fashion shops in London."

"How very interesting. What's the name of your clothing chain?"

"Stanhope Fashions. It's a family business. I inherited it from my father."

"It's very admirable of you to have kept the shops going yourself, Mrs Mitchell. It's always so much easier to hand the day-to-day operations over to someone else, isn't it?"

"Oh, I like to be fully involved. I spend most of my time at the Oxford Street branch. The others are in Kensington, Marylebone and Covent Garden, and they're all run by ladies I trust wholeheartedly."

"Does your husband help with the family business?"

"No, he's an artist."

"An artist? How fascinating. Anyone I might have heard of?"

"No. He doesn't spend a great deal of time painting these days. He teaches instead."

"Very interesting, all the same."

Given that Mr Mitchell was little more than an art teacher by the sounds of things, Thomas deduced most of the money lay on Mrs Mitchell's side of the family. This was presumably why she seemed so willing to employ the services of an expensive lawyer. She was keen to ensure that her interests were well protected.

He checked the clock on the wall. His next client would

be arriving shortly. "This has been a very informative opening conversation, Mrs Mitchell. Are you happy for Miss Watkins to arrange another so we can discuss your case in greater detail? I should like to allow plenty of time for us to discuss everything."

"Of course." Ellen smiled. "I feel happy to have made a start, at least, though I appreciate there's a lot to tell you and a lot more work to do."

"There will be, but you're in safe hands. I've managed countless divorce cases in the past, many of them involving large sums of money. May I ask whether there are any children in your marriage?"

"Yes, we have two daughters. They're still quite young, unfortunately. I do worry about the effect this will have on them."

"Naturally. Let's arrange another appointment, and then we can discuss how you wish to progress."

Chapter 8

ELLEN MITCHELL's legs felt weak as she stepped out of the offices of Bewick, Palmer and Curran on Cavendish Square.

I've done it. I've finally plucked up the courage to speak to a solicitor. She opened her umbrella in the light drizzle and made her way toward her shop on Oxford Street.

Twelve years of marriage.

Ellen felt sad that it was about to come to an end, but she simply couldn't endure it any longer. Not after her most recent discovery.

Walter would be extremely shocked when he received the solicitor's letter, but she still had time to accustom herself to that thought. She didn't want to be too hasty; she wanted every move to be as well-thought-out as possible. She was determined to ensure that he received none of her family's money and she needed to protect the children too. He would be shocked, but it was only right that he should pay the price for what he had done.

The Oxford Street branch of Stanhope Fashions was just a short walk from Oxford Circus. Ellen threaded her way through the lunchtime shoppers, umbrellas jostling for space above the busy pavement.

This flagship store always recorded the best takings. This was to be expected, given that it was located at the heart of London's busiest shopping district.

The shop had been here for as long as Ellen could remember. As a young girl she had visited the place with her father and she fondly recalled helping him count the money from the till at the end of each day. He had shown her how to record the takings and manage the stock. She had learned everything from him and, now that he had retired, he trusted her to run the business herself. She knew how proud he was of her. Ellen felt a lump in her throat as she considered how sad he would be to learn of her divorce.

She counted about a dozen customers in the shop as she entered. A couple of customers were admiring a fringed black dress on one of the mannequins. Sleeveless and low-waisted, it was beaded with sequins; exactly the sort of dress that would appeal to flappers.

Stanhope Fashions also catered to older women who were looking for something to wear for a special occasion. The prices were reasonable, so Ellen expected her shop girls to sell in volume. There were accessories to sell too: shoes, handbags, hats, headbands and fans. She frequently told her girls that they shouldn't be selling *dresses*; they should be selling *outfits*. Although her prices were mid-range, the service had to match that of an expensive boutique. It was what encouraged the customers to return. These were all principles her father had instilled in her and she intended to stick to them as diligently as possible.

Barbara was standing behind the counter while Lucy assisted a customer.

Ellen was just about to step inside her office when she

overheard Lucy saying: "If you'd like a bit more time to think about it, you could always come back later."

Ellen clenched her teeth. She positioned herself behind the counter and watched the interaction.

"I will, if that's all right," replied the dowdy lady in a floppy hat. "I'm not sure I want to spend quite so much money just now."

Lucy thanked the customer and said that she hoped to see her again soon. Ellen's teeth clenched even harder as she watched the dowdy customer leave the shop.

"Miss Briggs!" she snapped at the girl. "A word out the back, if you please."

Lucy's face fell, and she quickly followed her employer into her office.

"I'm sorry, miss," Lucy began. She was a petite young woman with dark hair.

"What should you have said to that customer instead?"

"She seemed so indecisive. I didn't want to force her to make a decision, but I should have offered to sell her some accessories and then discounted the overall price."

"Exactly. Customers will always use the price as an excuse to leave. We need to remind them they're getting something of great value. If they buy the dress, the shoes and the hat, we can offer them a price that can't be matched elsewhere. You know all this."

"I do, miss. I'm sorry."

"You've been drilled on how to persuade customers to buy. The very first thing you learned is that you must never make it easy for them to walk out."

"I realise that. I really am sorry, miss."

Ellen sighed. Lucy was one of her better girls. Customers liked her but she wasn't pushy enough.

"You have a lot to learn, young lady, especially in my best store. If you can't do a better job of persuading customers to buy, I shall have to move you over to one of the other shops. I'm sure you wouldn't like that because I happen to know that this is the closest store to your home. I can't imagine you'd like to spend all your wages on tube travel."

"No, I shouldn't like that at all. I'll try harder, Mrs Mitchell."

"This isn't the first time I've had to speak to you about this, Miss Briggs. I'll be watching you closely from now on."

"I'm so sorry, Mrs Mitchell. It won't happen again."

Chapter 9

A LIGHT DRIZZLE fell on Augusta and throngs of students as she made her way along Gower Street toward the Slade School of Fine Art. It was located on the campus of University College London in Bloomsbury. A columned portico came into view the moment she turned in through the campus gate and she saw that the stone university buildings were arranged around a quad.

After making initial enquiries, Augusta discovered that the Slade School was located within the building on the northern side of the quad. She found a porter sitting behind a polished desk in the small entrance hall.

"I'd like to speak to Elizabeth Thackeray, please. I understand she's a student here."

"And you are?"

"Mrs Augusta Peel, a private detective. I'm carrying out some important work on behalf of a law firm."

"Elizabeth Thackeray, you say? I'll need to check whether she's a student here."

Augusta waited patiently while he consulted a book on his desk. Two long corridors extended in opposite directions either side of her, and she could hear the faint sound of voices behind closed doors. A wooden staircase rose up to the floor above on the far side of the porter's desk.

"She's one of our second-year students," said the porter, "but you can't disturb her now. They're in the middle of lectures. You'll have to come back later."

"What time?"

"About twenty minutes."

Augusta bided her time by walking up and down Gower Street. She admired the imposing red-brick edifice of University College Hospital across the road. Students loitered outside a row of Georgian townhouses further down the street which suggested that the previously residential buildings had become part of the university.

Augusta had been forced to close the shop while she carried out this work. She thought of the customers who might be disappointed and would inevitably buy their books elsewhere. She had written a notice that morning saying, 'Help Wanted' but had forgotten to pop it in the window before she left.

The corridors were filled with students when Augusta returned to the art school. Some were carrying sketchbooks and many wore overalls over their clothes. Augusta decided to make her way along one of the corridors and keep asking people to point her in the direction of Elizabeth Thackeray until she found her.

Eventually, her luck came in.

"Over there," said a young man.

He pointed to a prim-looking woman with short, waved brown hair and round spectacles. She wore a buttoned-up, collared dress made from grey wool, and was clutching a sketchpad to her chest.

Augusta made her way through the crowd to speak to her. "Miss Thackeray?"

The young woman gave a cautious nod.

"My name is Mrs Augusta Peel. I'm a private detective."

Elizabeth's eyes widened.

"I've been tasked with investigating the whereabouts of Miss Catherine Frankland-Russell," continued Augusta. "She appears to be missing. Do you happen to know where she might be?"

Elizabeth gave a resolute shake of the head. "No, sorry. I can't help you." Her lips thinned, as if she wished to say no more.

"Have you seen her recently?"

"No, I haven't seen her at all."

"But you do know who I'm talking about?"

The young woman gave this some thought, then eventually said, "I knew her a long time ago."

"I understand that you were friends when you were young."

"I haven't seen her for years. I have no idea where she might be these days."

"She's somewhere in London, I believe. Have you seen her around here by any chance?"

"I've already told you I haven't. Now, I must go."

Augusta didn't want to pester Elizabeth any further, so she simply stood by and watched as the young woman walked away.

She seems rather evasive. Why?

Augusta remained in the corridor for a while. She noticed that Elizabeth didn't immediately hurry off. Instead, she lingered near a doorway, as if she were waiting for someone. She kept glancing over at Augusta, apparently uneasy that the private detective was watching her.

Who is she waiting for?

Augusta's question was swiftly answered when a man in his forties stepped out into the corridor. He was tall with a boyish, chubby face and scruffy brown hair and he wore paint-spattered overalls over his clothes. *A member of the teaching staff?* Augusta wondered.

She watched as the pair walked down the corridor together and were lost in the crowd.

Augusta felt disappointed. She had expected Elizabeth to be more helpful.

What's she hiding?

Chapter 10

A MOTORBIKE ROARED up a residential street in Marylebone later that afternoon. Elizabeth sat in the side-car, looking out for the right house. When she saw it, she gave the driver a sharp tap on the arm and the motorbike came to an abrupt halt, flinging her forward. She pulled off her goggles, hat and gloves before climbing out.

"I shan't be long," she said to the rider.

She walked up the steps of the neat three-storey house and knocked at the door. Her heart was pounding as she waited for a reply. *How will I be received?*

She surveyed the street. It appeared to be a wealthy neighbourhood and she deduced that Dorothy Cooper had married well. *But will Dorothy want to speak to me?*

"Elizabeth? Has something happened?"

Dorothy rose from her seat the moment the maid showed Elizabeth in. She was a few inches taller than Elizabeth and appeared well-groomed, with neat, fair hair and carefully applied rouge. Jewellery sparkled at her ears and throat, and she wore a turquoise dress of fine silk. Dorothy somehow seemed older than her now that she was married.

"I just wanted to let you know," began Elizabeth. "A lady came to see me today. She's looking for Catherine."

"Catherine?"

Elizabeth nodded.

"What did you tell her?"

"That I didn't know where she was."

"Did she ask anything else?"

"She said that Catherine was missing."

"Missing?"

"I didn't ask any questions. I just wanted to get away."

Dorothy seated herself at the parlour table and wiped her brow. "Does anyone know you're here?"

"Only Walter."

"Who's Walter?"

"My boyfriend."

"I heard a noisy motorbike out on the street just now. Is that how you got here?"

"Yes, it belongs to Walter. I travel in the sidecar."

Dorothy shuddered. "Dangerous things."

"If you say so."

"Did the woman who spoke to you give her name?"

"Augusta Peel."

Dorothy shook her head. "The name means nothing to me. What did she look like?"

"She was about thirty-five, possibly forty, with wavy auburn hair. Plain-looking clothes. She told me she was a private detective."

"A private detective? What would a private detective want with Catherine?"

"I don't know. Although I could make an educated guess."

"If that were the reason, she would have wanted to speak to you about it, too. I don't think it can be that. It must be something Catherine's got herself mixed up in."

"Have you seen her recently?"

"No. Anyway, you shouldn't be here."

"I know, but Mrs Peel's visit has unnerved me. I haven't heard Catherine's name mentioned for so long."

"Well, whatever it is, it's nothing for us to worry about."

"How do you know that?"

"Because otherwise that detective woman would have come for us as well, wouldn't she? Nobody has called here about Catherine aside from you. You could have written me a letter instead of coming in person, you know."

"What if someone else had read it?"

"I could have burned it."

"But how could I have been certain that no one else would read it before you did? I thought coming here myself was the safest option."

"How did you know I lived here?"

"I looked your husband up in the directory. You needn't worry, Dorothy. I'm going now."

Dorothy got to her feet. "I'm sorry if I haven't been very welcoming. It's just that... Well, we need to be careful."

"I know."

"How are you keeping?"

"I'm well, thank you. I'm a student now. At the art school."

"I'm sure you're destined to stay in education forever, Elizabeth. You really enjoy studying, don't you? I was never any good at it."

"But look at this lovely home you have. I'm sure you must feel pleased with what you've achieved."

"Yes, I've been quite lucky. All I need now is a family."

"I'm sure that will follow in due course."

"I hope so."

Elizabeth smiled. She had always got on well with Dorothy. It was a shame they still had to keep themselves apart. *Surely enough time has passed by now...*

She turned to leave. "I'd better not keep Walter waiting any longer."

"Is he from the art college as well?"

"Yes. He looks after me so kindly. I was attacked last week, and he was ever so good to me afterwards."

"You were *attacked*?" Dorothy brought a hand up to her face in shock.

"Yes. I don't know who it was. A man trying to have his way with me, probably. But I got away."

"But that's so scary!"

"I know. But Walter has promised to protect me, so I should be all right now."

"Good, I do hope so. I don't suppose you ever hear from the other two, do you?"

"No."

"Me neither. I suppose it's better that way. Look after yourself, Elizabeth."

Chapter 11

Augusta examined her copy of *A Tale of Two Cities* the following morning and wondered whether the grey-coated customer had read this particular Dickens novel. If not, he might be interested in reading it once she had reattached the cover.

She laid it out on her worktable which was well-lit by the sunshine that was streaming in through the frosted glass window. It was a vast improvement compared with the basement workshop where she had previously toiled, although she missed the rumble of tube trains beneath her feet.

Augusta decided to remove the book's broken spine. She had just begun to snip away at it when the bell on the counter rang. She put down her tools and headed into the shop.

A dark-skinned young man of about twenty stood on the other side of the counter. He wore spectacles and a tweed suit and he was carrying a newspaper under one arm. "Is the position still available?"

"You mean the sign in the window? I only put it there half an hour ago."

"Am I your first applicant?"

"Yes, you are!" Augusta laughed. "Do you have any experience of working in a bookshop?"

"I worked at Webster's, just around the corner from here. Do you know it?"

"Yes, I've visited it a couple of times." Webster's looked as though it had been in the bookselling business for many years.

"Mr Webster sold the business, and the new chap, Mr Fairburn, brought his own staff with him so I wasn't needed any more."

"I'm sorry to hear it."

The young man seemed polite and well-mannered. He appeared to be a promising candidate.

He peered into Sparky's cage. "You have a canary."

"I'm looking after him for a lady who's in hospital at the moment. He's called Sparky and he'll be very pleased that you didn't call him a budgerigar."

"I knew he was a canary straight away. My mother keeps them." He reached into his jacket pocket and pulled out a notebook and pen. "Mr Webster will be able to provide you with a reference for me."

"That would be very useful."

"I'll give you his address." He wrote down a Blooms-bury address in neat handwriting, then ripped out the page and handed it to her.

"Thank you." Augusta was already warming to this amicable man. "I'm Mrs Peel. Augusta Peel. May I ask your name?"

"Fred Plummer."

"It's nice to meet you, Mr Plummer. I could ask you

numerous questions about your bookselling experience but it would probably be best if you simply worked a few hours as a trial. What do you think?"

"I'd love to!" He smiled. "You've only just opened, haven't you? I'm sure this shop was sitting empty a few weeks ago. It used to be a magic shop, didn't it?"

"Apparently so."

"It's a very nice place," he commented, glancing around. "All the books are second-hand, are they?"

"Yes, they've all had previous homes. I've repaired a number of them."

Fred raised his eyebrows. "You repair the books yourself?"

"Yes, I quite enjoy it. That's what I was doing out the back just now when you rang the bell."

"I'm sorry for disturbing you."

"It's no trouble at all. I'm so pleased that you're interested in working here. How about I take the sign down from the window and you come along tomorrow morning to try out the position for a short while?"

"I'd like that very much, Mrs Peel. I'll see you then." Fred turned to leave. "I'm off to find somewhere warm to read this." He gestured at the newspaper beneath his arm. "Awful news about that murder, isn't it?"

"What murder?" Augusta had been too busy to read her newspaper.

"You haven't heard?" Fred returned to the counter and opened out the newspaper.

'Tragedy in Bloomsbury' read the headline. Beneath it, the subheading stated that a woman had been murdered in Torrington Square.

"Torrington Square?" exclaimed Augusta. "But that's near here!"

He nodded. "About ten minutes' walk. Dreadful, isn't it? She was a student at the university and just happened to be walking through the square yesterday evening."

Augusta froze when she saw the victim's name. "Elizabeth Thackeray," she said slowly. "Twenty-one years of age."

"That's no age at all." Fred gave Augusta a concerned look. "Are you all right, Mrs Peel?"

"I think so." She recovered her breath. "Actually, I'm not really. You see, I knew this young woman. Well, I didn't really *know* her but I spoke to her just yesterday. I had to speak to her about someone. If it's the same woman..."

She paused for a moment, her mind racing. *Is it possible that I'm mistaken? Or is this really the woman I spoke to just yesterday?*

Augusta read through the rest of the article, which confirmed that the victim had been a student at the Slade School of Fine Art. She felt a prickle in her eyes. "Oh, how sad. It has to be her. How desperately sad. Mr Plummer..."

"Call me Fred."

"Thank you, Fred. I hope this isn't impertinent of me to ask, but do you have any free time today? In fact, do you have any free time right now?"

"Yes of course. What can I help you with?"

"Would you mind looking after the shop for an hour or two? I need to go and speak to a friend of mine. He's a police officer."

"Yes, absolutely. That's fine with me, Mrs Peel. You go and do what you need to do."

Augusta spent a few moments explaining how to make a sale. She knew she was taking a risk leaving her shop in the hands of a young man she had only just met, but there wasn't a great deal of money in the till and she instinctively felt that she could trust him.

"Thank you, Fred."

"Don't you worry, Mrs Peel. Sparky'll keep an eye on me."

Chapter 12

AUGUSTA MANAGED to cover the distance between her shop and the scene of the crime in just five minutes. Despite its name, Torrington Square was a long rectangle, lined on either side by tall Georgian townhouses.

A crowd of onlookers had gathered and a length of rope, guarded by several constables, had been strung across the road to keep them away from the crime scene.

"Is Detective Inspector Fisher here?" Augusta asked one of the police officers.

"I don't know."

"Are there any inspectors from Scotland Yard here?"

"Yes, Scotland Yard are here, but I don't know which inspectors they sent."

"I'm a private detective and I work closely with Detective Inspector Fisher. I recently met the victim and I'd like to help. Could you please let me through?"

The officer conferred with a colleague who then walked briskly off up the square.

"He's gone to ask," the officer explained to Augusta.

"Thank you."

Why would someone want to murder Elizabeth Thackeray? Augusta felt a shiver down her spine. The poor girl was just a harmless young student.

The constable soon returned with Philip.

"Augusta! Come on through."

She ducked under the rope and joined him. "Elizabeth Thackeray," she said hurriedly. "Do you recall the name? She was the woman Hugh Farrell suggested I speak to about Catherine Frankland-Russell. I met with her at the art school just yesterday."

Philip's eyes widened. "Really? No wonder you hurried here. I hadn't realised it was the same woman. What did she tell you?"

"Very little. In fact, she seemed rather evasive. I asked her about Catherine, but she told me she hadn't seen her for a long time. Then I saw her walk off with a man who appeared to be a teacher."

"That may well have been Walter Mitchell," said Philip. "From what we've learned of Miss Thackeray so far, they seem to have been having an extramarital affair."

"He's married? Oh dear. Where was she found?"

"On the lawn, over there beyond the railings." He pointed to a spot where a group of police officers were huddled beneath a cluster of bare-branched trees. "Either she was walking through that little strip of parkland or he pulled her into it. She was found by a couple of fellow students at about seven o'clock, and we know that she left the art college at half past five. So she must have been attacked within that short period. A post-mortem is being carried out today, but from our initial observations she appears to have been strangled with a ligature. Attacked from behind, we think, so she would have been taken by surprise. There were signs of a struggle, but the poor girl didn't stand much of a chance."

"How horrific."

"Yes, it's despicable. She was making her way home after a lecture. She had a room at a lodging house in Keppel Street." He pointed behind them. "Just three hundred yards from where she was attacked. We haven't found anybody who saw or overheard the attack, nor have we found anyone who saw a man lurking around or running away."

"And what of Walter Mitchell?"

"I'll be interviewing him later this morning. He's our chief suspect at the moment, as you can imagine. Sometimes when a married man has an affair, he decides he wants to put an end to it. Then the mistress threatens to tell his wife and he loses his temper."

Chapter 13

"I DIDN'T HURT ELIZABETH! I'd never do such a thing. I didn't even know it had happened until I arrived at work this morning. That was the first I'd heard of it! Can't you give me time to grieve? I don't understand why you want to ask me questions about it. I can't believe you would even think that I might have done it!"

Walter Mitchell slumped over the table and clamped his palms over his eyes. He was sitting in a spartan interview room at Hunter Street police station in Bloomsbury opposite two police officers: one an inspector from the station and another from Scotland Yard.

How can they treat me this way, knowing how upset I am?

"No one has made any suggestion that you were responsible for Miss Thackeray's death, Mr Mitchell," replied the Scotland Yard inspector. He'd told Walter his name was Inspector Fisher.

"When did you last see Miss Thackeray?" asked the other inspector. He had bushy brown whiskers and went by the name of Harris.

Walter sat up. "Just before her last lecture of the day. I

suppose it was about half past three." He looked down at his hands then picked a dried spatter of red paint from his jacket sleeve.

"You last saw Miss Thackeray at half past three yesterday," Inspector Harris said. "At the Slade School of Fine Art, was it?"

"Yes, in the corridor on the first floor. It was only a brief encounter. Just a greeting, really."

"How did she seem when you spoke to her?"

"Just like Elizabeth." He shrugged. "Normal. It wasn't as if she knew she was about to die." His voice choked and he looked up at the officers. "Are you aware that she was almost attacked a week ago?"

Inspector Fisher's eyes narrowed. "No, we weren't aware of that. What happened?"

"Exactly the same sort of thing. She was on her way home, walking through Gordon Square. A man tried to grab her, but she got away. I told her not to walk in those dark, lonely places at night, but for some reason she liked doing it. I thought she would stop after the attack last week. She told your lot about it, but nothing was done!" He stared accusingly at the men opposite him.

Inspector Fisher put on a pair of spectacles and made some notes. "Did you hear anything about the attack, Inspector Harris?"

"No, I didn't. You said that she spoke to the police, Mr Mitchell?"

"Yes. She ran out of the square and found a couple walking close by. They helped her summon a constable, who took down all the details. It wasn't far from here! He must be based at this station. He should have done something about it, shouldn't he?"

Inspector Harris made some notes. "I shall have to check with my men to find out which of them spoke with

Miss Thackeray last week. I'm quite sure he would have carried out a thorough search of the area."

"You should have more men on the street, Inspector! They need to be out on the beat, ensuring that this sort of thing doesn't happen!"

Inspector Fisher furrowed his brow. "The fact that Miss Thackeray was attacked twice suggests one of two things. Either she was particularly unlucky, or the same assailant was determined to harm her. I'm tempted to lean toward the latter theory. Do you know of anybody who might have wanted to harm her, Mr Mitchell?"

"No, absolutely not. I would have dealt with him if I had!"

"I take it she was quite shaken up after the first attack?"

"Yes, for several days, but she was pleased that she had managed to get away. I think it made her confident that if she could get away so easily there was nothing to worry about! How many men do you have out there, looking for this maniac?"

"We've plenty of men working on the case, Mr Mitchell. We'll catch him soon enough."

Walter didn't like the way Inspector Harris stared at him as he said this.

"You said that you didn't think anybody was after Miss Thackeray," said Inspector Fisher, "but did anything unusual happen recently? Did she seem particularly upset by anything or anyone?"

"No." Walter shook his head, but as he did so, he recalled something. "Actually, yes! A woman came to the school and spoke to her yesterday. Said she was a private detective and asked her about an old friend. Elizabeth didn't like that at all."

"Did she explain why?"

"No, not really. Then she insisted I take her to a

friend's house in Marylebone. I have a motorbike, you see, and she often travels in the sidecar."

"This visit to the friend was connected to the conversation she'd had with the private detective, was it?"

"I think so. I couldn't think why else she would want me to take her there all of a sudden."

"Had you ever taken her to meet that particular friend before?"

"No! It was all news to me. I just waited outside on my motorbike. She was only in there for about ten minutes."

"What was the name of this friend?" asked Inspector Fisher.

"Dorothy Cooper."

"And the address?"

"Manchester Street in Marylebone. Number twenty-three, I think it was."

"You say that she wasn't in there for long. Did she tell you what they discussed?"

"No, but I think the lady detective's appearance at the college prompted the visit. I really don't know anything more than that."

"Interesting," responded Inspector Fisher.

"Does your wife know about your affair with Miss Thackeray?" asked Inspector Harris.

"No!" Walter felt a lurch in his stomach. Ellen thought he was currently teaching his class as usual. How was he going to hide this mess from her? "She can't find out about it."

He regarded the sceptical expressions on the faces of the two men opposite. "Oh, I guess that I may have to tell her... She'll be extremely upset. I suppose I'll have to explain that I've been speaking to you today, but..."

Walter's stomach turned and he looked down at his

hands again. It felt as though everything had fallen in on him. He had to pick his way out of the rubble somehow.

"How is the relationship between you and your wife at the moment?" asked Inspector Fisher.

Walter felt a snap of anger. "I take offence at the personal nature of that question, Inspector!"

"If you were engaged in an affair with a student, I imagine it was because your relationship with your wife was not particularly good."

"How impertinent!"

"But true, nonetheless? Mr Mitchell, if you want us to find out who murdered your girlfriend, you'll need to be a little more helpful."

"But you're asking me about my marriage, which has nothing to do with what's happened to Elizabeth. That man'll be out there murdering more women unless you crack on and find him. I don't see how spending all day questioning me is going to help."

"Where were you between the hours of five and seven yesterday evening, Mr Mitchell?"

Walter clenched his teeth. He decided that showing any sign of anger would get him nowhere. *They won't let me out of this miserable room until I've answered all their petty questions.* He let out a long sigh, then said, "I was in my office at the university and then I went home."

"What time did you arrive home?"

"I can't remember exactly. I usually get back at about half past six."

"Your wife was already at home at that time, was she?"

"Yes, she was."

"And where is your home?"

"Great Titchfield Street."

"Over on the other side of Tottenham Court Road,"

said Inspector Fisher. "Not far away, then. How did you get there?"

"On my motorbike. It takes me about five minutes."

"In that case, if you arrived home at half past six yesterday evening, you probably left your office at about twenty-five minutes past six, would you say?"

"Probably nearer twenty past six. Not that a few minutes here or there matters, but I suppose you want me to be precise. I would have left my office at about twenty past and then I would have gone to my motorbike outside and started it up. Then I would have driven home in about five minutes."

"When we ask your wife what time you arrived home, she'll be able to confirm that it was about half past six, will she?"

"Yes, probably. I'll need to have a proper think about the exact time because you've put me on the spot here. I can't remember exactly now."

Walter's brain felt foggy. The more he talked, the less he remembered. *Why is my heart pounding so quickly? I can barely remember a thing.* He was sure that the police suspected him.

"How was your relationship with Elizabeth Thackeray?" asked Inspector Harris. "Was she happy?"

"Yes."

"She was content to share you with your wife, was she?"

"I think so."

"You *think* so? You don't know?"

Walter took a deep breath and tried to calm himself. "She wanted me to leave my wife."

"And did you intend to?"

"I hadn't really considered it."

"Don't you think that a little odd?"

"No, why?"

"It suggests to me that you had no intention of ever leaving your wife and that Miss Thackeray was disappointed by this."

"I don't know!" He scratched at his scalp. *Why can't they just leave me alone?*

"Was she pregnant, by any chance?" asked Inspector Harris.

"No!" He thumped the table. "What a question!"

"I'm sure you understand why we needed to ask it."

"No, I don't understand why you would need to ask it! You should be out there trying to find the man who did this!"

"We already are, Mr Mitchell. But can you see why you might appear to be a suspect?"

"No, I can't! Everything was fine until this happened!"

"I don't think everything really was fine, was it?" said Inspector Fisher.

"All right, then, it wasn't perfect. But someone attacked Elizabeth and it *wasn't* me! I can barely even believe it's happened." He pushed his thumb and forefinger into his eyes in a bid to stem the tears.

"You said you were in your office until twenty past six," said Inspector Harris. "Can we speak to anyone who could confirm that?"

"I don't know."

Walter groaned and slumped his head down onto the table again. He felt exhausted. He didn't know what to say to these men anymore, and his memory was getting muddled. *Was I really in my office until after six o'clock?* He couldn't remember.

Chapter 14

"WELL, it's not every day you get called into a police station," said Walter breezily as he stepped inside the drawing room that evening. He smoothed down his ruffled hair and clothes, as if brushing himself off after a fight.

Ellen regarded her husband from her position on the sofa and wondered if he was ready to be honest with her. She folded up the fashion magazine she had been reading and placed it on the table next to her. "Was it about the murder of that girl? She was one of your students, wasn't she?" Ellen had seen the newspapers that morning and made the connection.

"Yes. It's very sad." Walter strolled over to the drinks cabinet and poured himself some sherry from a crystal decanter.

His mood appeared nonchalant, but Ellen couldn't see how he could be so blasé when something so serious had just happened to one of his students.

"Do you want one?" he asked, holding up the decanter.

She felt her lip curl in response to his false cheer. "No, thank you."

"Are Doris and Agatha upstairs?" he asked, slumping into the chair opposite her.

"Yes, they're with Judy."

"Good, good. I don't want them overhearing us." He took a gulp of sherry.

"Why were you called into the police station?"

"They wanted to interview me. Can you believe that one of them was an inspector from Scotland Yard? Scotland Yard! This is clearly a serious business. I had to find someone to teach my classes at the last minute."

"Did they want to speak to you about the murder?"

Walter rested one ankle on the opposite knee and examined his sock. "Yes, because she was one of my students. I think I may have taught her a few times last year, but I didn't know her well. It's difficult to remember who's who with so many students there!" He gave a little laugh, seemingly in the hope that she might join in. "They're interviewing everyone, of course."

"Everyone in the entire university?"

"No, just at the art school. And not everyone there, either. That would take forever! Just the staff and a few of the students. The ones who knew her, I suppose. They couldn't possibly interview all the students. How long would that take? Months!"

Ellen could tell that he was waffling now, and she noticed how quick he had been to deny knowing the girl. *How stupid does he think I am?* "Surely the police must have had a particular reason to interview you," she ventured.

"No particular reason, no. They're interviewing lots of people, as I said. They interviewed Miss Collins, too. She was just arriving as I was leaving."

"I have no idea who Miss Collins is."

"She teaches sculpture." Walter looked at his watch, clearly feeling he had done enough in the way of explaining himself. "I suppose I'd better get changed for dinner."

"There's no hurry," she responded. "Tell me about the girl who was murdered. Why would someone want to kill her?"

"I have no idea whatsoever. It's awful! She was just walking home after her lectures. She was a second-year student, I believe. She certainly didn't deserve that."

"I read in the paper that her name was Elizabeth."

"Yes, I believe so. Elizabeth Thackeray." Walter gazed into the bottom of his empty glass.

"I suppose you're going to get yourself another drink now."

"Does it matter if I do? A terrible thing has just happened, Ellen, and I've had to answer to the police about it."

"Do they think you did it?"

"Of course not! But they have to suspect everyone to begin with, don't they? And when you're sitting in a room with them, they do a very good job of making you feel guilty, even though you're not. They'd suspect *you* if you worked at the art college, too."

"Would they? But why on earth would I want to murder a student?"

"Well, obviously you wouldn't, but then neither would I. They just suspect everyone don't they?" He got to his feet and poured himself another drink.

Why can't he just be truthful with me? How much longer is he going to keep stringing out these lies? Is he really a suspect in Elizabeth's murder? Did she threaten to reveal the affair and make him snap?

Ellen had scheduled another meeting with the solicitor. She wasn't sure when to break the news about the divorce to Walter. She wouldn't be able to do it for a few days now, as he was clearly upset about what had happened to his girlfriend. *If only I had made my mind up about the divorce sooner. Why didn't I plan things better? I'm married to a man who has just been interviewed by the police about a murder. What will happen if people find out?*

"You mustn't tell anyone about this," she said. "You realise that, don't you?"

"I've nothing to hide." He returned to his seat.

"You may have nothing to hide but you know the way people think. The moment they learn that the police have spoken to you, they'll assume there must be some sort of evidence. It wouldn't look good."

"Wouldn't look good in what sense?"

"For the reputation of our family! If this becomes widely known, customers will start asking questions when they visit my shops."

"Why does everything have to be about your reputation and your customers?"

"It doesn't. I just don't want people asking questions."

Walter took a large swig from his glass. "I'm obviously an embarrassment to you."

She glanced at his messy hair and paint-spattered clothes. "You're not an *embarrassment* to me," she lied. "I just need to make sure that the business isn't affected by all this. And as you've already pointed out, you're completely innocent, so there's no need for it to be affected. But you know how rumours spread and how people talk. One word that the police have spoken to you will be enough to set the gossips off. Please just keep it under your hat for now, and I'll do the same."

I'll have to hurry the divorce along now. The longer I'm associated with this man, the greater the risk that my name will be pulled into it. And what if the police decide he's guilty? I'll have to change my name and start all over again. What a mess!

"It's also for the sake of the children, Walter. Don't even mention it to the house staff. You know how the children overhear things the servants say."

"And just pretend that a young woman hasn't died?"

"No one has to pretend that it didn't happen, but she didn't really mean anything to us, did she?"

Now's his chance to confess. Ellen stared at him, awaiting his response.

He avoided her gaze and ran a hand though his hair. "No. She meant nothing at all."

Chapter 15

"THAT'S A GOOD DAY'S TAKINGS," said Augusta, closing the cash register. "Thank you, Fred. You've been extremely helpful today. I'm so very pleased that you walked into my shop this morning!"

She walked over to the door, locked it and turned the sign to 'Closed'. It was already dark outside. "Do you think you might like to come back tomorrow?" she asked as she returned to the counter.

"I'd be delighted to."

"Thank you. I may be quite busy with other work following recent events, so I'll need someone to help look after this place."

"I'm more than happy to help, Mrs Peel. Does your work have anything to do with the murder?"

"Yes. For some reason I've found myself doing a little detective work alongside running the shop. I had anticipated a quiet couple of weeks at first but a few unexpected things have happened recently. If you're happy to proceed, perhaps we can consider the trial to have been a success and you can become an official employee."

Fred gave a broad grin. "How exciting, Mrs Peel! But don't you want to pursue that reference from Mr Webster before you make a decision? You only have my word for it."

"I'll certainly contact him, but I can already see that you're more than capable of holding the fort here, Fred. And besides, I trust you."

Augusta hoped she was right on this score.

"Thank you," he replied. "I've enjoyed today."

"Good."

"And Sparky sang earlier. I didn't recognise the tune, but I enjoyed it all the same."

"It wasn't 'Don't Dilly Dally on the Way', then?"

"Can he sing that?"

Augusta laughed. "No, but I'm sure he'd give it a good go."

They both noticed a movement by the door.

"Looks like there's a late customer," said Fred.

A face peered in through the glass and Augusta recognised it as Philip's.

"It's Detective Inspector Fisher," she explained, going over to unlock the door for him. "Philip!" she said, inviting him in. "Meet my new shop assistant, Fred Plummer."

"Nice to meet you, Mr Plummer." Philip walked into the shop, leaning on his stick as he went. "You certainly didn't waste any time with your recruitment, Augusta."

"Fred found me, really. He's been a big help today."

"That's good. You'll need some help with this place."

"Is it all right if I go home now, Mrs Peel?" asked Fred.

"Yes, of course. I'll see you tomorrow."

"He seems like a nice lad," said Philip once Fred had left.

"He is, and he did extremely well today. I had to leave him to it."

"That was very trusting of you, Augusta. He could have emptied the till and run off."

"He could have, but he didn't. And I suspected that he wouldn't."

"The shop looks good," he said, surveying the shelves. "If only I had more time to read." He glanced over at the door behind the counter. "And you've also got your hide-away out the back there."

"My *workshop*."

"Isn't that the same thing?" He smiled. "Sparky looks settled, too." He pushed a finger between the bars of the birdcage and waggled it. "He doesn't seem very interested in me."

"That's because you don't have any food. Here." Augusta pulled a bag of bird seed out from behind the counter. "You can give him something to keep him going until teatime if you like."

"How many meals does he have a day?"

"Four."

"*Four?* It's not bad being a canary, is it?" Sparky nibbled at the seed while Philip rested against the counter. "Seeing as I was working nearby today, I thought I'd drop in to let you know how we got on. The post-mortem confirmed that Miss Thackeray was strangled with a ligature... most likely a piece of rope. It wasn't left at the scene; the murderer appears to have taken it away with him. The odd thing is, she was also attacked last week, in Gordon Square."

"Really?"

"Yes. I hadn't realised that until we spoke to Walter Mitchell this afternoon. He told us about the attack and that it had been reported to a constable at the time. After the interview, Inspector Harris from Hunter Street station spoke to the constable in question and he confirmed that Miss Thackeray had indeed reported the crime to him last week. A number of constables searched the place but found nobody there."

"Could it have been the same man both times?"

"Either that or the girl was terribly unlucky."

"Was she able to give a description of her attacker after the first incident?"

"She wasn't able to tell the constable a great deal as it was dark at the time. The attacker pushed her to the ground from behind, apparently, but she managed to get away and run out of the square."

"It's a shame she didn't get a good view of him."

"Yes, a huge shame. Someone else may have seen him, however. E Division are busy knocking on doors as we speak, asking people about both incidents."

"Gordon Square is quite close to Torrington Square, isn't it?"

"Yes. Torrington Square sits about one hundred yards south-west of Gordon Square, so the locations of the two attacks are very close indeed, and both are en route to Miss Thackeray's home in Keppel Street. The assailant didn't take any jewellery or belongings, and her clothing was left undisturbed."

"In which case, the motive was unlikely to have been robbery or anything more sinister."

"Exactly. It seems the killer wanted her dead and nothing more. At the present time, I'm tempted to believe that it was the same man who attacked her on both occasions. She got away the first time but was sadly unable to escape the second time round. There have been no other reported attacks on students in the area recently."

"What did Walter Mitchell have to say for himself? Do you think he could have done it?"

"It's difficult to tell after just one conversation. He seemed genuinely upset about her death but that doesn't mean he didn't murder her. He may have changed his mind about their relationship and wanted her out of the way, or perhaps she had threatened to tell his wife about the affair. The post-mortem revealed that the girl wasn't pregnant. Sadly, that has been the reason for similar murders in the past. I couldn't quite get the measure of Walter Mitchell. He mentioned you, however."

"Did he?"

"Yes. He said you'd visited Elizabeth at the Slade School."

"That sounds about right. I did stand about watching her for a while. I feel rather bad about it now as she must have found it rather unnerving, but I wouldn't have done so if she had been more forthcoming."

"Well, your visit seems to have prompted an urgent action on her part as she subsequently paid a visit to a friend of hers called Dorothy Cooper. Mr Mitchell didn't appear to know anything about Mrs Cooper – he's never even met her – but apparently he drove Elizabeth to her house, and she was in there for about ten minutes."

"Did Elizabeth tell him what the conversation was about?"

"Apparently not. All we have is Mrs Cooper's name and an address. I wondered if you might like to go and speak to her?"

"I suppose I could give it a try. Is she aware of Elizabeth Thackeray's death yet?"

"It's been all over the newspapers today so I'd be surprised if she wasn't. But I suppose it's best to be mindful of the possibility that she hasn't yet heard the news. It looks as though I'm pulling you into an investigation once again, Augusta."

"One I was already partly involved with, I suppose. But I'm feeling rather worried now, Philip. Do you think Miss Thackeray might have been murdered because I went to speak to her?"

"Why would she have been?"

"It's a bit of an odd coincidence, don't you think? I asked her about Catherine Frankland-Russell and found her evasive in her answers, as if she were hiding something. Then that very same evening she was murdered!"

"It may just be a coincidence and nothing more."

"But what if it isn't? What if someone silenced her because she really did know something about Catherine?"

Chapter 16

"I LIKE THE COLOUR," said the red-haired customer as she twisted around on her toes to survey the deep-blue evening dress in the mirror from every possible angle. "I'm just not so sure about the fit."

"We can adjust it for you," responded Lucy, aware that Mrs Mitchell was within earshot. "Where would you like it to be altered?"

The customer continued to look in the mirror. "I think it needs a lot of adjusting. It would most likely become a whole new dress altogether."

"The cut is lovely and straight," said Lucy. "A very fashionable look at the moment."

"Yes, I suppose it is. But I'm afraid I'm not a terribly fashionable woman."

"Perhaps you could become one."

"Perhaps. But once you've become a little set in your ways, it can be difficult to change them. I know I should probably try to wear a dress like this but I simply wouldn't feel comfortable in it."

"How about making it into a whole outfit rather than just a dress?"

The lady frowned. "What do you mean? Spend even more money on something I don't feel comfortable in?"

If Mrs Mitchell hadn't been in the shop, Lucy would have happily let the customer change out of the dress and go on her merry way. She did not enjoy adopting such a pushy approach.

"We could offer it at a discount," Lucy said, stepping over to a colourful hat display. She picked up a dark-blue cloche hat with a beaded silk ribbon around it, carefully placing it on the customer's head. "Don't you think the dress looks better with a matching accessory?"

The red-haired woman pushed out her lips as she considered this. Before she could respond, Lucy placed a blue feathered fan in her hand.

"Now you have a full outfit," she said. "And we have some lovely silk shawls that would match."

"Really? I do like the idea of a shawl to cover my shoulders."

Lucy found one with fine golden threads woven into it which shimmered in the light. She could see that the customer was beginning to look more impressed.

"The fit of the dress looks better now," the woman said, twisting around again.

"It fits you perfectly. It's just a case of accustoming yourself to a different cut from the style you usually wear."

After a short negotiation about the discount, the customer left with the full outfit, along with a necklace she had spotted on display at the counter.

Lucy felt relieved to have made the sale.

"That was very good, Lucy," said Mrs Mitchell. "You listened to me and did what I asked."

"I do try to do my job well, miss." Lucy couldn't afford

to lose her job. She was completely reliant on it to keep a roof over her head, even if that roof belonged to a drab lodging near Regent's Park.

It was a quiet morning in the shop, so once the customer had left, Barbara opened a newspaper on the counter, pushed her spectacles up her nose and began to read.

"Are there any updates about the murder?" Lucy asked. She had scarcely believed the news when she saw it the previous day. "I read that she was a student at the Slade School of Fine Art. That's where your husband works, isn't it, Mrs Mitchell?"

Her employer's lips thinned. "Yes, that's right."

"Did he know her?"

"I believe he taught her in the past." Mrs Mitchell's face was rigid.

"They haven't caught the killer yet, have they?" asked Lucy.

"Not as far as I know," Ellen replied. "Put that newspaper away now, Barbara. We don't want customers walking in and seeing you reading it. That hat display could do with a bit of rearranging, Lucy," she added. "The displays need to be changed regularly to keep the store interesting for our regular customers."

"Of course." Lucy walked over to the hat display and began to remove the hats. Once she had done so, she started putting them back in new positions. She decided to group them by colour rather than by style this time.

She stifled a yawn. She had barely slept a wink the previous night for thinking about the murder. *Was it a random attack? Or did someone intentionally murder Elizabeth Thackeray?*

Lucy was desperate to find out more. She had hoped that Mrs Mitchell might have heard something of note from her husband, but her employer didn't seem interested in talking about it. In fact, there was something unusual about the way she was refusing to talk about it. Usually when such a terrible incident occurred, people wanted to discuss it. Those who remained silent often knew more than they were letting on.

Chapter 17

Augusta stood in the hallway of number twenty-three Manchester Street, waiting for the housekeeper to return. A mahogany grandfather clock ticked away steadily. The walls were wood-panelled and a colourful carpet runner led up to the staircase. Dorothy Cooper and her husband seemed to occupy the entire building which meant they were wealthy. Augusta was well aware that many large London townhouses were being converted into more affordable flats these days.

The housekeeper, a plump lady in a navy dress, emerged from a doorway to Augusta's right. "Mrs Cooper has requested more information," she said. "What is it you wish to ask her, exactly?"

"I'm investigating the murder of Elizabeth Thackeray, who I believe was a friend of Mrs Cooper's. I'm assisting Scotland Yard with their inquiries. We want to find out as much as we can about Miss Thackeray as it's possible that she knew her assailant. A vital clue to his identity may lie in her recent activities."

The housekeeper nodded, then disappeared back

through the door. A short while later she returned to tell Augusta that Mrs Cooper had agreed to see her.

Dorothy Cooper was seated in her parlour at a table covered with a lace tablecloth. She had fair, bobbed hair and wore an apricot-coloured day dress. She regarded Augusta warily as she entered the room.

"Please accept my condolences on the death of your friend, Mrs Cooper," said Augusta.

"Thank you." Dorothy gave a weak smile and gestured for Augusta to sit. "She wasn't a close friend, just someone I knew many years ago. How can I help?"

"Thank you for agreeing to see me. I understand that Miss Thackeray paid you a visit just a few days ago."

A flicker of surprise registered on Dorothy's face. "How did you know that?"

"The information was passed to me by Scotland Yard. They asked me to come and have a chat with you."

"Am I in trouble?"

"No, not at all. I'm just trying to find out everything I can about Miss Thackeray in the hope that we can find out who committed this awful crime. It's thought that perhaps her attack wasn't a random act, you see. We think someone may have been after her specifically."

"Oh, that's awful." Dorothy looked down at her hands in her lap. "When she told me about the first attack she was convinced it was a man who was trying to…" She shifted in her seat. "Well, you know…"

"I know what you mean."

She looked up at Augusta again. "I don't think she believed someone was actually after *her*. She just thought she was in the wrong place at the wrong time. It's an awful shame she wasn't able to get away the second time."

"How long had you known Elizabeth?"

"Since we were girls. Our families knew each other, but we didn't really remain firm friends. We rarely saw each other."

"What was the reason for her visit the other day?"

Dorothy opened her mouth a little, then closed it again. "She said she was just passing."

"I understand she was brought here by a friend of hers, Walter Mitchell. They just happened to drive along this street, did they?"

Dorothy shrugged. "I suppose so."

"I suspect there was a reason for Miss Thackeray's visit, Mrs Cooper, and it's important that you tell me what it was. We really need to find out who did this to her."

Dorothy looked down at her hands again. "I really can't recall a specific reason. She was only here for ten minutes or so. The housekeeper will be able to confirm that."

"Did Miss Thackeray seem worried about anything?"

"No, I don't think so. In fact, she seemed quite happy to be out with her boyfriend."

"Did he come inside the house at all?"

"No, he didn't. He waited outside." She looked up at Augusta. "Do you think he did it?" she asked. "It does happen, doesn't it?"

"It does indeed. The police are investigating all possibilities as we speak. But I notice you still haven't told me what it was that Miss Thackeray came here to speak to you about."

Dorothy bent her head again.

"I don't know you very well, Mrs Cooper," said Augusta. "In fact, I don't know you at all. But judging by your manner, I deduce there's something you're not telling me. Miss Thackeray clearly had a reason to visit you a few days ago. You said yourself that you hadn't seen each other for quite a while. What was it she came to speak to you about?"

Dorothy bit her lip, then looked up at the ceiling. She appeared to be grappling with her thoughts.

What could her secret be?

"Fine, I shall tell you," she said sullenly. "She came to see me because you had unnerved her. She told me you visited her at the Slade and spoke to her after a lecture. She didn't know who you were, and neither do I, for that matter. It wasn't nice to just turn up and speak to her like that."

Augusta felt relieved that she finally seemed to be getting somewhere. "I'm saddened to hear that my sudden appearance at the art school unnerved her. That certainly wasn't my intention. I didn't find Miss Thackeray particularly talkative. Perhaps if she'd allowed a little more time for discussion she would have realised that my visit was nothing to worry about at all. She did appear to be hiding something from me, and I would venture to say that you're doing the same thing, Mrs Cooper. Your business is your own, of course, but I really would appreciate your help in finding out who did this to Miss Thackeray. I'm very sad that she was worried by my visit. Am I really so intimidating?"

Dorothy smiled a little. "No, you're not intimidating, Mrs Peel. It wasn't *you* that upset Elizabeth. It was what you *said*."

"What did I say that upset her?"

"You asked after Catherine Frankland-Russell. She doesn't like talking about Catherine, you see. They fell out a long time ago and she tended to find any talk of her upsetting."

"I see. Perhaps I should have explained that I had been

asked by Miss Frankland-Russell's family to locate her. Did you happen to know Miss Frankland-Russell, by any chance?"

Dorothy paused briefly before replying. "Yes, we both knew her. A long time ago now. Neither of us have anything to do with her these days. Why did Catherine's family ask you to find her?"

"They've had no contact with her for some time and they're worried about her. Her parents are extremely keen to hear that she's safe and well, as am I. I only spoke to Miss Thackeray because I was looking for Miss Frankland-Russell. And now Miss Thackeray is no longer with us, which is desperately sad. I didn't know her but, having spoken to her just a few days ago, it's very difficult to accept that this has happened to her. So I'm now trying to find out two things: where Miss Frankland-Russell is and who murdered Miss Thackeray. Anything you can do to help me would be much appreciated, Mrs Cooper." Augusta fixed her eyes on the young woman, hoping Dorothy could see how keen she was to have her help.

Dorothy sighed. "I last heard news of Catherine from mutual friends. That would have been about a year ago now, as it was shortly before I got married. I heard she was working at a shop in London."

"Thank you," said Augusta with smile. "That's a great relief. I was worried about her well-being but it sounds as though she's probably safe and well. You've been extremely helpful, Mrs Cooper. Do you happen to know what type of shop it is or where it might be situated?"

"All I know is that it was a clothes shop on Oxford Street. She may not even work there anymore. Someone mentioned it to me, but I can't even remember who it was now. It was during a day out at Kew Gardens. A whole group of us went there."

"A clothes shop on Oxford Street, did you say?"

Dorothy nodded.

"Thank you, Mrs Cooper."

Augusta concluded that Mrs Cooper evidently wasn't going to divulge the real reason for Miss Thackeray's visit but at least there was a glimmer of hope. A clothes shop on Oxford Street. The street was a mile long and consisted of little other than shops. Rather a vague lead but certainly better than nothing.

Chapter 18

HAVE I SAID TOO MUCH?

Once Augusta had left her home, Dorothy began to worry that she had given away more than she should have. *But what else could I have done?* It would have been difficult to lie to Mrs Peel, she seemed the sort of lady who could spot lies quite easily.

What will she tell the police?

The housekeeper, Mrs O'Reilly, had shown Mrs Peel out before heading down to the kitchen where she was preparing lunch for one o'clock. That meant Dorothy had half-an-hour to herself. She wondered whether that would be enough to carry out the plan she was formulating in her head.

She stepped out into the hallway and crept past the ticking grandfather clock. Then she made her way up the stairs, avoiding the ones that creaked. Sneaking about her own home like this seemed foolish but she was determined that no one else should find out what she was up to. Mrs O'Reilly was a little nosy at times and there was always a risk of her mentioning something she had seen to Dorothy's husband.

Reaching the landing at the top of the stairs, Dorothy turned and made her way past her bedroom, dressing room and a guest room. Then she climbed another flight of stairs up to the second floor. After that, she was able to move about more easily as there was little chance of Mrs O'Reilly hearing her from the kitchen down in the basement.

The final flight of steps up to the attic was a narrow staircase with a thin carpet runner. Before the war, the rooms at the top of the house had been occupied by live-in servants. These days, Dorothy and her husband used the rooms for storage.

The smaller of the two rooms contained Dorothy's old belongings. Trunks and tea chests were stacked along one side of the wall and a rocking horse she had loved as a child stood beneath the window. She stroked the horse's mane, smiling as she recalled the many times she had done the same thing as a young girl. She had planned to find someone who could give the horse a fresh lick of paint and fix its broken ear. Then it would be perfect for her own children to play with in the future.

She turned to the stack of luggage and pulled out a leather trunk. She dusted it off, set it down on the floor and opened the clasps.

The trunk was crammed full of mementoes from her schooldays: notebooks, sketches, diaries, certificates and rosettes. There was even a small silver cup she had been awarded as reading champion. Dorothy eventually found a large, tatty envelope filled with photographs. She couldn't resist taking one last look at them. She spotted herself in a photograph of the school lacrosse team; the one sport she had really excelled at. Another photograph showed her knitting socks for soldiers with her school friends.

She felt a heavy sadness the moment she saw Elizabeth in the photographs. Only two days had passed since her old friend's visit and now she was dead.

How can it be so?

It had to have been an opportunistic attack. Although that's what Elizabeth had thought after the first time. *Did the same person attack her the second time?* If so, perhaps Dorothy also had something to worry about.

She picked up the trunk and carried it into the other attic room. This room was larger and overlooked the street. Beyond the window, a gusty wind was whisking the clouds across a grey sky. Dorothy gathered up the contents of the trunk and began throwing them into the fireplace.

Where are the matches?

There was no box on the mantelpiece. She dashed down the narrow stairs to fetch the matches from the fireplace in her bedroom, hoping all the while that Mrs O'Reilly wouldn't come up from the kitchen at the worst possible moment and see what she was doing.

As she returned to the attic room, Dorothy saw her personal items lying in the fireplace once again. She felt a lump in her throat.

I have to do this. People have started asking questions. I've worked really hard to the hide the truth for so long. All the evidence has to go.

Holding back a sob, Dorothy lit a match and dropped it in among the papers and photographs. There was an instant whoosh of flame.

However, the smoke didn't go up the chimney. Instead, it billowed out into the room.

The chimney was blocked.

Cursing, Dorothy ran over to the sash window and tried to push it up. It hadn't been opened in some time so the frame was jammed. She struggled for a minute or two and eventually forced it open.

I have to get rid of everything!

Bending down, she scooped up more papers and photographs from the trunk and threw them into the fireplace. She tried to fan the smoke toward the window but it simply whirled around the room, stinging her eyes.

Have I made a terrible mistake?

The windowpane rattled as a strong gust of wind blew in, causing some of the papers to be whipped out of the fireplace. They landed on the hearthrug, which, to Dorothy's horror, caught alight. She stamped out the flames with her foot, grabbed the poker and tried to keep everything in the fireplace so it would quickly burn away.

She paused to grab the last few papers from the trunk and it was only then that she noticed the flames in the corner of the room. A scrap of burning papers had landed there without her noticing and one corner of the floorboard was alight.

The smoke was growing unbearable. Dorothy knew that if she closed the window she would choke, but the breeze from the window kept scattering the papers out of the fire.

There has to be something else I can do to save the situation.

Dashing downstairs once again, she headed for the bathroom where there was a jug and running water. It wouldn't be long before someone else noticed the fire. She would have to be quick.

But, by the time she returned to the attic room, three small fires were alight. Eyes stinging from the smoke, she poured water on one but there wasn't enough to tackle the other two. The smoke had reached the back of her throat, making her gag and choke.

Dorothy staggered back toward the door.

The fire was out of control.

Chapter 19

"CATHERINE FRANKLAND-RUSSELL once worked in a clothes shop on Oxford Street," Augusta said to Philip in his office at Scotland Yard. "At least, that's what Dorothy Cooper told me."

"Interesting! Do you know if she still does?"

"No."

"Did she tell you the name of the shop?"

"I'm afraid not."

"Any other clues about it?"

"None."

"It'll be quite a task to find the right one, then. I'll see if I can get some men on the case. We really need to determine whether Miss Thackeray's death had anything to do with Miss Frankland-Russell."

"I'm worried that someone may have decided to silence Miss Thackeray after I spoke to her about her missing friend."

"Shall we find out what the lawyer makes of it?"

"Thomas Bewick?"

"Yes. He's the one who got you involved in all this in

the first place, isn't he? I think we need to tell him what's happened and see if we can find out why someone might not want Catherine Frankland-Russell to be found."

"How nice to see you again, Mrs Peel," said Thomas Bewick as Augusta and Philip stepped into his elegant office. "Ah, you have a colleague with you this time."

"Detective Inspector Philip Fisher from Scotland Yard," announced Augusta.

"An inspector from the Yard!" The lawyer gave an impressed nod as he shook Philip's hand. "Delighted to meet you, Inspector. Do please take a seat, both of you."

The pair made themselves comfortable on one of the plum-coloured sofas.

"Is there any news of Miss Frankland-Russell?" asked Mr Bewick, sitting himself opposite them.

"We think she may be working in a clothes shop on Oxford Street," replied Augusta. "An old friend of hers gave me the information."

"Really?" His eyebrows lifted. "That's wonderful news! In which case, she clearly hasn't come to any harm."

"We can't be completely certain of that just yet, but it is hopeful news. Now it's just a case of finding her."

"And with a bit of luck, that should be quite quick, shouldn't it?"

"With a bit of luck, yes. Although there are rather a lot of shops on Oxford Street."

"There are indeed. Thank you for this new information, Mrs Peel. I shall telephone Lord Frankland-Russell as soon as we're finished here and tell him the promising news."

"I'm sure he'll be happy to hear it, and hopefully we'll

have more to tell him shortly. In the meantime, I'd like to ask you a few more questions, Mr Bewick, because something very unpleasant has happened since I began my investigations into Miss Frankland-Russell's whereabouts."

"Oh dear."

"You've no doubt heard about the recent murder in Torrington Square?"

"Yes, I have. A horrible business. The victim was a student at the university, I believe."

"Her name was Elizabeth Thackeray," replied Augusta, "and I spoke to her shortly before her death. Apparently, she knew Miss Frankland-Russell."

"Did she now? What was she able to tell you about her?"

"She didn't tell me very much at all but I suspected she was hiding something. And now she has suddenly lost her life."

"At the moment we suspect that Miss Thackeray was deliberately targeted," said Philip, "and there is some concern that Mrs Peel's conversation with Miss Thackeray may have had something to do with her death. Perhaps Miss Frankland-Russell, or someone who is protecting her, was worried that Miss Thackeray would give away her whereabouts. It's just a theory, but I'd be interested to hear if there's anything further you can tell us about Miss Frankland-Russell's disappearance."

Mr Bewick ran a hand through his grey hair thoughtfully, then shook his head. "No, I can't think of anything. I can't see why anyone would go to such desperate lengths to stop Miss Frankland-Russell from being found. I can't imagine many people even knew that Mrs Peel had spoken to Miss Thackeray."

"There's nothing about Miss Frankland-Russell or her

family that concerns you at all?" asked Philip. "Connections with any unsavoury characters, for example?"

"Goodness, no! Lord and Lady Frankland-Russell would never associate themselves with anybody of that sort. Then again, perhaps I'm making assumptions. I can only tell you what I know, I'm afraid."

"It's a real puzzle," said Philip. "Miss Thackeray seemed very reluctant to give Mrs Peel any useful information about Miss Frankland-Russell. Then she went to discuss the matter with an old friend, after which she was murdered. Perhaps I'm looking for a link when there isn't one, but it does seem to be a strange coincidence."

"Absolutely," responded the lawyer. "It does seem rather odd. I would normally suggest that you speak to Lord and Lady Frankland-Russell directly, but I'm under strict instruction to manage all communications with the family myself. Lord Frankland-Russell is not a well man, you see. He suffers from great stress to his nerves; something that I'm sure will be alleviated as soon as he discovers the whereabouts of his daughter. I'll speak to him on the telephone shortly and will put it to him that someone doesn't want her to be found. Let's see what he says. He may be able to tell us something useful or he may not. I must say, I'm impressed that you managed to track down one of Miss Frankland-Russell's friends, Mrs Peel. That's more than I managed."

"Maybe so, but I'm concerned that I might have inadvertently brought harm to Miss Thackeray."

"I can understand that worry, but I'm sure it's entirely unfounded." He turned to Philip. "I do hope you catch the individual who did this despicable thing, Inspector. Best of luck with your investigation."

· · ·

Augusta and Philip stepped out into Cavendish Square with the wind tugging at their overcoats.

"We're only a short walk from Oxford Street," commented Philip. "Do you fancy making some inquiries about Miss Frankland-Russell at a few of the clothes shops?"

Augusta checked her watch. "It really can only be a few, I'm afraid. I've left Fred in charge again for most of the day. He must think me a very negligent bookshop owner."

"I'm sure he doesn't think that."

They turned into Holles Street, the junction with Oxford Street lay just a short walk ahead of them.

"Walter Mitchell is still our most likely suspect," said Philip, "so I don't think you need worry that you're in any way responsible for Miss Thackeray's death, Augusta. It's not good for your peace of mind."

"No, it's not."

He stopped and turned to face her. "Then promise me that you'll stop worrying about it."

"All right."

"That's not a promise! I really want you to put it out of your mind."

She met his gaze. "All right, I promise. But it's difficult—"

"Of *course* it's difficult, but you mustn't blame yourself. Now, I'd like to focus my attention on Walter Mitchell a bit more closely. I think the next logical step is to speak to his wife. How do you fancy being the scribe for the interview?"

Augusta smiled. "I'd love to."

Chapter 20

"W<small>ALTER</small>?"

He jolted at the sound of his name. Opening his eyes, Walter realised he was slumped over the bar with his head resting on his hands. It took a fair bit of effort to lift his head and focus his eyes on the person who had spoken his name.

"Are you all right?" It was Digby Rayburn, the life-drawing lecturer. He was a thin, lean man of about sixty, and he wore a neat tweed suit.

"I think so." Walter sat up on his stool and took a sip of his beer.

"Shall I get you another?"

"Thank you."

Walter recalled calling in at the Orange Tree pub after work. The pub stood close to the art school, on the corner of Euston Road and Gower Street. It wasn't something he did often but he had felt the need to calm his troubled thoughts.

"What's the time?" he asked Digby.

"Just after eight."

"Oh no," he groaned. Ellen would be angry with him for returning home so late.

Digby picked up the two pints of beer he had just been served. "How about we move to a more comfortable seat? I can see you falling off that stool."

"Fall off it? Why would I fall off it?" Walter felt the room sway like a ship at sea as he stood to his feet. He followed Digby over to a table beside the frosted glass window, knocking into a chair as he went.

"I suppose you must still be in quite a bit of shock," Digby said as they sat down. "It's such an awful thing to have happened to that poor girl and they haven't even caught the chap who did it yet. I don't suppose it'll be easy to catch him, either. She was attacked in the dark and it could have been just about anyone, couldn't it? I hope they get him soon, though. A lot of our female students feel very unsafe now. They've taken to walking about in groups and I can't say that I blame them."

"She thought it was safe," responded Walter, staring into his drink. "She wasn't worried about walking around on her own. Even after she was attacked the first time."

"I didn't know anything about that! It had happened to her before, had it?"

"Yes, about a week ago."

"Poor girl." Digby tutted. "There really are some dreadful scoundrels around these days. We ought to be doing more about it, don't you think? The police seem too busy to go out on the beat regularly. Perhaps we could get a group of chaps together to patrol the streets around the university. That would make the ladies feel a lot safer."

"That sounds like a good idea."

"You seem terribly cut up about it, Walter. I hope you don't think I'm imposing, but I heard that you knew Elizabeth Thackeray rather well."

Walter noticed a small fly in his drink. He plunged his finger in and fished it out. "Yes, I did. She really didn't deserve to die." He wiped the drowned fly onto his trousers and took another gulp of beer, some of it dribbled down his chin. *Is it sensible for me to drink even more?*

"Nobody deserves to be murdered," mused Digby. "It's awful. I should hate to be murdered!"

"I told her to be careful after the first attack. I offered to drive her home, but she didn't want to put me out. She liked walking through the squares at night and we had to be careful about being seen leaving anywhere together. There was a risk people would talk." He noticed how slurred his speech had become. *Am I making any sense?* "I think some people knew anyway, so I suppose I'll be in trouble about it at some stage. That's all I need."

Digby nodded. "You're quite right, Walter. A good few people knew about it."

"They think I murdered her, don't they?"

"Oh, good grief, no! I don't see why anyone would think that."

"Well, the police think I did it. Only because they can't find anyone else though."

"You're in quite a tricky position, aren't you? It's not as if you can openly grieve for her. I suppose that would make matters rather complicated with your wife."

"Ellen doesn't know anything about it but I had to tell her I was interviewed by the police. She didn't like that at all. She probably thinks I did it as well."

Digby began to fill his pipe.

Walter didn't know his colleague particularly well, but he decided he liked Digby's company. He was a calm, mild-mannered man and didn't seem judgemental. "Let me buy you a drink, Digby."

"If you insist. Are you sure you want another?"

"Oh, yes. I definitely need another."

Walter returned to the table a short while later with two pints of beer and a damp patch on his trousers from where he had spilled one of them.

"I'll have the one that's got less in it." He clumsily pushed the other over to Digby who was puffing away on his pipe.

The conversation turned to work and they discussed various colleagues and some of the amusing things their students had done. Walter even managed to forget about Elizabeth and his wife for a short while. Then the two men fell into an easy silence and everything came flooding back.

"Elizabeth told me something once," he said. "I suppose I can say it now that she's dead."

"Don't feel you have to," responded Digby with a frown.

"No, I will, because it's an awful thing to feel like you're carrying something around. Sometimes you just have to tell someone about it to make it easier."

"If you say so."

"I do. A problem shared is a problem halved. That's the saying, isn't it? I wish she hadn't told me but what's done is done. She told me not to tell anyone, but none of that matters any more. Would you like to hear it, Digby?"

Chapter 21

ELLEN MITCHELL HAD EXPECTED to be approached by a police officer with a bullying attitude. Instead, she found Detective Inspector Fisher quite a pleasant man to speak to. He was fairly handsome, with dark, greying hair, and eyes that narrowed thoughtfully as he listened. She noted that he had a walking stick and wondered why. He was accompanied by an auburn-haired woman called Mrs Peel, who looked to be about forty. Mrs Peel didn't say a great deal but she had a notebook with her and regarded Ellen curiously.

Ellen smoothed her hair and pretended not to be nervous. She didn't appreciate being interviewed by Scotland Yard. *What does Elizabeth Thackeray's death have to do with me?*

She was having a hard enough time with Walter as it was. He had returned home the previous night more intoxicated than she had ever seen him. Once this interview was over, she would go back to see the solicitor again and forge ahead with the divorce. She'd had enough.

"Thank you for meeting with us today, Mrs Mitchell," said the inspector.

"I really don't know how I can help you," she replied. "I never met Elizabeth Thackeray."

"I understand. As you can imagine, this is a rather difficult case. A young woman was murdered in a park at night-time and we have no witnesses. Unfortunately for us, and for you, it means we're having to interview just about anybody and everybody in an effort to determine what happened to her that evening. You're probably aware that we've already interviewed your husband."

"Yes. He told me that a number of staff and students at the Slade School were being interviewed."

"That's right." The inspector shuffled uneasily in his chair. "This isn't easy for me to say, Mrs Mitchell, but I can't beat about the bush. In order for us to speak honestly and frankly, I must break the news to you that your husband had rather a close friendship with Elizabeth Thackeray."

Ellen assumed an expression of surprise. "Friendship? What do you mean by that?"

"I mean exactly what I said, Mrs Mitchell." He gave Mrs Peel a sidelong glance, as if appealing to her for help. She responded with a shrug, as if she didn't know what to add.

The inspector turned back to Ellen. "I can only repeat what other people have told me, but I have learned that a unique friendship existed between your husband and this particular student."

"Do you mean they were having an affair?"

"That's another way of putting it."

Ellen gave a loud sniff and made a show of bringing her fingers up to her nose, as if she were attempting to hold back tears.

"That's why we were particularly keen to interview him," continued Inspector Fisher in a softer tone. "What I wished to determine by talking to you, Mrs Mitchell, was whether you were aware that such a friendship, or *affair*, as you put it, was taking place."

"No," Ellen lied, determined to distance herself from the girl. If she admitted that she had known about the affair, they might consider her a suspect. She couldn't risk that. "I knew nothing about any friendship between them. In fact, I knew nothing of the victim until I read about the murder in the newspaper. Then my husband happened to mention that a student at his college had been murdered. He told me he was being interviewed along with everybody else but he never explained that there was a particular reason for it. Now that I've been made aware of the reason, I must say that it's all the more distressing to me, Inspector, as I'm sure you can imagine." She pulled a handkerchief out of her handbag and buried her face in it.

There was a short pause while the inspector and his assistant respectfully waited for Ellen to recover herself.

"I see," he said eventually. "I do apologise that I've had to be the bearer of bad news today, Mrs Mitchell. I imagine you'll need some time to think this over and discuss it with your husband. I was only interested to hear whether you knew about the relationship or not."

"No, I knew nothing of it!" she wailed. "I thought our marriage was a happy one!"

"I'm very sorry to hear it. I wonder, Mrs Mitchell, whether you might be able to recall the events of the evening Miss Thackeray died? It was three days ago now. Can you remember what time your husband returned home from work that day?"

"The usual time, I suppose."

"May I ask what the usual time is?"

"About half-past six, or sometimes as late as seven."

"And on that particular day?"

She gave this some thought. "Yes, it was half-past six. I feel quite sure of it."

"Thank you, Mrs Mitchell."

"Are you asking me to provide an alibi for him?"

"Your account certainly provides an alibi for him from half-past six onwards."

"What time was the girl murdered?"

"Sometime between five and half-past five, we think."

"Are you suggesting that he might have murdered her before he came home?"

"We're not suggesting that at all, Mrs Mitchell. We're just trying to establish alibis for everyone connected with Miss Thackeray, where possible."

"Then you'll need to obtain an alibi from someone at the college for earlier in the evening."

"Yes, absolutely. May I ask what your own movements were that evening, Mrs Mitchell?"

The directness of this question made her flinch. *Is he accusing me?* "I need an alibi as well, do I?"

"I'm not asking for an alibi, as such. I'm just interested to know what you might have been doing that evening."

"Do you think I might have had something to do with the murder? Even though I had no idea who the victim was?"

"I would really appreciate it if you could simply answer my question, Mrs Mitchell. What were you doing in the early evening that day?"

"I was at my shop until six o'clock, and then I took a taxi home."

"Where is your shop, Mrs Mitchell?"

"It's on Oxford Street."

"And you left at six o'clock?"

"Yes. We're closed for customers from half-past five and then there's the usual sorting out to do afterwards. I got a taxi back and arrived home at six o'clock. I sometimes walk if it's a nice evening but at this time of year it usually isn't. We live in Great Titchfield Street, so the journey only takes five minutes by car."

"I see. And the other people who work in your shop can verify your account, can they?"

"You *are* asking for an alibi, Inspector!"

"We make a point of asking this question in every interview, just in case we ever need to follow something up. I'd really appreciate your cooperation, Mrs Mitchell. This is no easy task for the police, and we're very keen to get hold of this man before he causes anyone else any harm."

Ellen decided to comply. After all, he was probably just following procedure. "Lucy and Barbara were working with me that day. They'll be able to confirm that I was there at the time Miss Thackeray was murdered."

"Very good. What's the name of your shop, Mrs Mitchell?"

"Stanhope Fashions. I run four shops under that name. It's a family business."

"What do you sell?"

"Ladies' fashions."

"Very interesting, I shall have to tell my wife. She very much enjoys shopping on Oxford Street. I'll ask her to call in." He gave a charming smile which Ellen found rather disarming.

"Please do, Inspector. I should be very pleased to see her in my shop."

Mrs Peel leaned forward and spoke for the first time. "I don't suppose you've ever employed a young woman by the name of Catherine Frankland-Russell, have you?"

"No, I haven't."

"Have you ever heard the name before?"

"No. Who is she?"

"Just someone I've been looking for," Mrs Peel replied.

Chapter 22

Augusta stepped into Stanhope Fashions and admired a sequinned evening gown on its mannequin.

"I liked the display better the way it was before," one of the shop assistants said to the other.

"I wanted to arrange it by colour," came the reply.

"I think customers choose a style before they think about colour."

"Well, I'm inclined to think that they choose the colour first."

"What does Mrs Mitchell think about it?"

"I suppose we'll find out when she gets back from the lawyer's office."

"She's had a lot of meetings with her lawyer recently. What do you suppose that's all about?"

The shop girls noticed Augusta. "Can I help you?" asked the dark-haired one. "What are you looking for today?"

There was little doubt in Augusta's mind that she was Miss Frankland-Russell. With her bobbed hair and large, dark eyes, she closely resembled the young woman in the photograph Thomas Bewick had shown her.

"I need a new blouse," she replied, "but it seems you only sell evening wear in here. These dresses are very beautiful." She glanced around, then smiled. "I don't have many occasions when I get to wear anything like this, unfortunately."

"Perhaps you could persuade your husband to take you somewhere nice?"

"There's a good idea. I could try, couldn't I?"

A customer entered and distracted the other shop assistant. Augusta observed them for a moment, then moved closer to Lucy. "Do you mind me asking your name?"

"It's Miss Briggs. Lucy Briggs."

Augusta glanced around the shop again before replying, her voice lowered. "Is Lucy your real name?"

"Yes." She fixed her gaze but her voice sounded feeble.

"I'm not convinced that you're telling the truth. I have a strong suspicion that your real name is Catherine."

Lucy's mouth opened and closed a few times, as if she were trying to find some way to deny it. Augusta felt a little guilty about confronting her, having taken the young shop assistant completely by surprise.

"My name is Lucy Briggs," she replied. "I don't know what you're talking about. Are you interested in buying something?"

"Yes, I am." Augusta turned to the hat display. "I should like a new hat." She reasoned that if she bought something, the young woman might be more inclined to speak openly with her. "I like this green one here." Augusta wasn't sure where she would ever wear it but she hoped she would have a reason to go somewhere special one day. She picked it up, tried it on and admired herself in the mirror. "Yes, I'll take this one. Thank you."

"You made your mind up very quickly," commented Lucy.

"I tend to make my mind up quickly when it comes to buying clothes. I don't particularly enjoy shopping, you see."

Augusta continued to look at herself in the mirror. When she saw the young woman looking over her shoulder at her, she said, "Your parents are very worried about you, you know."

Lucy's complexion paled.

"They would really like to hear from you," Augusta continued.

"Please don't tell anybody you've seen me here."

"Why not?"

"I had to get away from them. If they find out where I am, they'll force me to get married."

Augusta was beginning to understand why Catherine had cut contact with them. "Don't you want to get married?"

"Yes, I should like to be married one day. But there's a particular man they want me to marry and I refuse to have anything to do with him."

Augusta gave this some thought. Catherine Frankland-Russell clearly didn't want to be found, yet her parents were worried about her. *What am I to do?*

She turned to the young woman and spoke as quietly as possible. "Perhaps we can meet later to discuss this. I'm a private detective, and I was asked by your family's lawyer to track you down, so I'm obliged to tell him where you are. However, before I do so, I'd like to hear your explanation. Would you be willing to meet with me?"

"Only if you promise not to tell them where I am."

"I won't say anything for the time being; you have my word on that. Where would be a good place to meet when you finish work today?"

"Outside St Peter's Church," she replied. "It's close by, on Vere Street. Do you know it?"

"I'll find it."

"I'll see you there at six o'clock."

"Thank you," said Augusta. She hoped the young woman would turn up. "Now, how much do I owe you for this hat?"

Chapter 23

St Peter's was a simple brown-brick building with a stone porch. Augusta waited on the steps of the church with her torch on so Miss Frankland-Russell would be able to spot her easily.

Once the bell struck six, she began to grow impatient. *Will she turn up?* Augusta had almost given up hope when the young woman hurried up to the steps.

"Sorry I'm late. Mrs Mitchell wanted us to do some tidying in the stockroom after we closed. I got here as quickly as I could."

"I appreciate you coming to meet me."

"How did you find out who I was?"

"I spoke to some of your friends. One of them was a girl named Elizabeth Thackeray. Do you remember her?"

Catherine gave a slight nod, then looked down at her feet. "I read about her death in the newspaper. I still can't believe it." She looked up at Augusta. "Why would someone want to attack her? Who would do such a thing?"

"That's what we're trying to find out."

"*We?*"

"I'm assisting Scotland Yard with their inquiry. I spoke to another of your friends, too. Dorothy Cooper."

"I knew her as Dorothy Henderson, but I heard she was married."

"It was Dorothy who said that I might find you in one of the clothes shops on Oxford Street. She wasn't enthusiastic about giving me the information; it took a bit of persuasion. Both Elizabeth and Dorothy seemed reluctant to talk about you, in fact. Do you know why that might have been?"

The young woman shrugged. "We fell out. That's all there is to it."

"May I ask what you fell out about?"

"I can't remember the exact details now. We were young and we all went off to do different things. I suppose we just didn't have much in common anymore." She paused. "Can you tell me why my parents are looking for me? I came back to London to get away from them. I can't believe they've gone and sent someone out to search for me. They must have had a change of heart, anyway, because the last time I spoke to them they wanted nothing more to do with me."

"When was that?"

"I suppose it was nearly a year ago now. We had a terrible falling out about the man they wanted me to marry. My parents are wealthy but they haven't given me a penny since we fell out, so I've had to fend for myself. Had I done what they wanted, I suppose I could have been living a better life by now. But I find myself working in a shop instead."

"Why did you change your name?"

"My real name was so distinctive. I knew that people would ask questions about my family and wonder why I was living independently from them. It just felt easier to create a new identity for myself."

"Why didn't you want to marry the man they had in mind for you?"

"He's absolutely vile! He's a good deal older than me, for a start, and my parents were only interested in the match because he's so wealthy. I couldn't see why they wanted me to marry into money when they already had enough, as far as I could tell. But that's exactly what they wanted, and they didn't care in the slightest what I thought about it."

Augusta could sympathise with this. "It seems rather old-fashioned to persuade your daughter to marry a man you've chosen for her."

"Oh, it is. My parents are very old-fashioned."

"Do you mind me asking who it was they wanted you to marry?"

"Someone called Mr Farrell."

"*Hugh* Farrell?" Augusta thought of the revolting man she had met when she first began looking for Miss Frankland-Russell.

"Yes. Do you know him?"

"I've only met him once but I can see why you wouldn't want to marry him."

"I'm pleased you agree. Where did you meet him?"

"His name was given to me when I began my search for you, so I went to his home to see if he happened to know where you might be. Could your parents really insist on you marrying him if they were to find out where you are?"

"They can't force me but I'm assuming the reason they sent you to find me is so they could try again. I don't want to have to endure that a second time! Please don't tell them you've found me, Mrs Peel. I just want to be left alone!"

Is it really fair to tell her parents where she is so they can pressure her into marrying a detestable man? Augusta wasn't sure she could bring herself to do it. *If I can persuade her to contact them herself, surely that's the best possible solution.*

"Perhaps you could write a letter to your parents to inform them that you're safe and well but they need not contact you. I'm sure that would reassure them, and you needn't tell them where you are or what you're doing."

Catherine sighed. "I'll think about it. But if they've gone to such great lengths to ask a lawyer and a private detective to find me, I suspect they'll find a way to track me down before long."

All Augusta could do was hope the young lady standing before her would decide that writing a letter to her parents was the best course of action. She appeared to have spoken quite honestly so far, but Augusta still sensed an evasiveness about her reasons for falling out with Dorothy Cooper and Elizabeth Thackeray.

"I don't suppose you have any idea why someone would have wanted to murder Miss Thackeray, do you?" she asked.

"No. As I've already told you, I hadn't seen her for a long time. I really don't know why he did it. Anyway, I must be getting on now."

"Of course. Thank you for meeting with me, Miss Frankland-Russell."

"Can I trust you not to tell my parents where I am?"

Augusta paused to give this some thought. She wanted the girl to trust her but could she give Miss Frankland-Russell her word? "Please do think about writing them a letter. I'll give you a few days to consider it and, in the meantime, I promise not to tell them or the lawyer where you are."

"How did it go?" asked Philip when Augusta joined him in the Woodstock public house close by. They were seated in a wood-panelled booth and the air was thick with tobacco smoke.

"We can't tell her parents where she is. They want her to marry that awful Hugh Farrell."

"The chap you poured that cup of tea over?"

"Yes, him. I felt rather sorry for her, quite honestly. I can fully appreciate why she wanted to get away from them."

"But surely they can't actually force her to marry him?"

"Who knows what hold they had over her in the past? I suppose we should be happy that we've found her safe and well. Although she has to work hard in a shop now and doesn't earn a great deal of money, she has her independence, at least, and she's not in any danger."

"Hopefully you'll be able to tell her parents that and they'll be content just to hear that she's safe."

"But what if Mr Bewick insists on telling them her exact whereabouts?"

"He already knows she works in a clothes shop on Oxford Street, so I should think her parents know it, too. He did say that he would inform them."

Augusta felt a pang of regret. "I wish I hadn't told him that now. I did so before I realised she was trying to escape her parents."

"You weren't to know the reason behind her disappearance, Augusta. You undertook the assignment based on the understanding that you were being paid to help find their daughter. That gives you an obligation to tell the lawyer where she is, does it not?"

"But I feel so sorry for her! She just wants to be left alone. She's entitled to that at twenty-one years of age, isn't she? I told her it would probably be best if she wrote them a letter to reassure them. I said I'd keep quiet about her whereabouts for a few days while she considers the idea."

"A few days? The lawyer will want to know as soon as possible that you've found her. That's what you agreed."

Augusta couldn't deny that Philip was right, but why couldn't he see that the poor girl deserved some sympathy? "Yes, I realise that's what I agreed to do but I'd assumed I was searching for a girl who was in danger, and who would want to be found or rescued. In hindsight, I realise that was a foolish assumption."

"It does seem a little foolish. Perhaps you should have asked more questions before taking the case on."

His patronising response made her teeth clench. "Perhaps I shouldn't have got involved in the first place! I didn't really want to. I'm trying to run a bookshop! I'd much rather be there than chasing around London after lost causes."

"You are helping, Augusta."

"Helping who?"

"You're helping me with the investigation into Elizabeth Thackeray's murder."

"I can't really see what I've done to help with that."

"You're good at this, Augusta."

She felt a snap of anger. "Actually, I don't think I am. Do you know what annoys me more than anything? People being evasive and not telling the whole truth. All three young women clammed up when I asked them about one another. There's something not right there but I have no idea how I'm ever going to get to the bottom of it. I'm reaching the point where I don't even think I care."

"You don't mean that, Augusta."

"I do! I really can't be bothered with it anymore. You're the police inspector, Philip. You sort it out with all the men you've got to help you. You don't need me, and I don't really want to be here."

She drained her drink, picked up her handbag and left the pub.

Augusta had only walked a short distance down Oxford Street when she heard Philip's voice behind her. "Wait!"

She turned to see him hobbling toward her.

"I can't run after you," he said as he approached. "Thank you for stopping. I've just had a thought."

"What is it?"

He stopped next to her. "What if Miss Frankland-Russell murdered Miss Thackeray?"

"Miss Frankland-Russell?" The idea seemed preposterous to Augusta. "I can't imagine her doing anything like that."

"As you said yourself, there seems be something very secretive about the relationship between these three young women. Maybe Miss Frankland-Russell is hiding from someone other than her parents. Perhaps Miss Thackeray said too much. And maybe Mrs Cooper knows something, too." He rubbed his brow. "Oh, I don't know. Perhaps it was just a silly notion of mine. Let me help you hail a cab, Augusta. Then you can head home and rest."

Chapter 24

WALTER MITCHELL DECIDED to avoid the pub when he finished teaching for the day and instead made his way straight home. He wanted to find out how Ellen had fared in her interview at Scotland Yard. He wasn't sure why they had wanted to interview her but his biggest concern was that they might have mentioned the affair.

He found his wife in a sombre mood in their drawing room. Dressed in a rose-coloured jacket and skirt, she was seated in her easy chair with a glass of sherry in her hand.

"How did it go?" he asked.

"It was a waste of their time. I didn't even know the girl. I learned a few interesting things while I was there, however." Her green eyes fixed on him, unblinking.

Walter sensed he was in trouble. He cleared his throat and sat down on the settee, trying to appear as good-natured as possible in the hope that it might improve her mood.

"What did you learn?" he ventured.

"That you didn't quite tell me the truth about Elizabeth Thackeray."

He knew that he had two choices. He could either admit to the affair or continue with his denial. *What exactly did the inspector tell her?* He clasped his hands together. His palms were clammy.

"So, are you ready to tell me the truth?" she asked.

"The truth is… The truth is that Elizabeth Thackeray and I got along well. I taught her, as I mentioned to you. We found ourselves bumping into each other occasionally, and we had conversations that were quite engaging. I don't usually have engaging conversations with my students, you see… We sometimes bumped into each other outside of lectures, and we got along well then, too. At the time you and I, well… We weren't getting on so well, were we? Things have been a little frosty between us for some time, and Elizabeth was someone I could easily chat to about things. I wasn't in love with her, let me make that perfectly clear! I wasn't in love with her at all."

"I see." His wife's face remained stiff.

What's she thinking? What's she about to say?

The silence in the room was almost unbearable. Walter felt compelled to continue talking, just to fill the void. "Obviously, it's all come as rather a shock, this news of her death. I don't know why anyone would do that to her… It's truly dreadful. But she was just someone I got along well with, nothing more. She would no doubt have met a charming male student before long and forgotten all about me. I suppose I was like a father figure to her." Walter laughed a little at this, then wondered why. He didn't know what to do with himself.

Ellen stared at him a while longer, then shifted her gaze to her drink. "I've spoken to a lawyer about obtaining a divorce," she announced.

This felt like a blow to Walter's chest. He held his

breath and stared at her. His wife of twelve years. The mother of his children. *Surely she's not serious?*

"Why?"

She lifted her eyes to him. "You were quite content to spend time with someone else. Doesn't that say it all?"

"No, I wasn't content. It was a foolish mistake. You can't petition for divorce! What about the children? What will your family think?"

Walter couldn't believe she would really consider such a thing. Ellen was normally so concerned about her reputation. People would talk and she hated people talking. She couldn't abide being associated with any sort of scandal.

"When did you speak to a lawyer?" he asked.

"I've spoken to him a few times now."

"You've been considering this for some time, have you?"

"Yes, while you were off gallivanting with that girl. You'll need to find yourself a lawyer as well."

"But how? Where would I find a lawyer? You can't just spring this on me, you know. It's been an awful few days. You can't even begin to understand what I've been through, Ellen. Please don't do this to me. Not now. This is a rash decision you're making. Give yourself a bit of time to think about it. The news you received from the inspector obviously wasn't what you wanted to hear. I'm so sorry you had to hear it from him. In hindsight, I should have explained it all to you myself. I should have told you I had been friendly with Elizabeth. It really wasn't anything much. It wasn't at all serious. What about the children?" His voice tailed off, tears welling in his eyes. "Not the children, Ellen."

"Perhaps you should have thought about the children before you decided to become so friendly with Miss Thackeray."

"But that was nothing! She meant nothing to me, Ellen. Not like you do."

"That's all very easy for you to say now that it's over and she's dead."

"Things had started cooling off before she died, anyway. I was just a foolish man who had fallen for the charms of a younger woman, and only very briefly. We've been married for twelve years, Ellen! We can't allow a moment of foolishness on my part to take all that away from us. You really must think carefully about this. When you do, I'm sure you'll realise that pursuing a divorce would be a very rash decision indeed."

"There's nothing rash about it, Walter."

Her expression was cold. She looked like her mother. Walter knew her parents had never approved of him. It had always been an uphill battle to prove that he was worthy of Ellen's affection. And now he had ruined everything through his own stupidity. He had got carried away with himself, thinking the affair would never really come to anything. He had felt sure that Elizabeth would eventually leave him for someone else, and he would have been happy with that because he had a wife to go back to. He had never anticipated all this.

He got up and went over to her chair. Kneeling beside her, he took her hand in his.

She pulled it away.

He looked up into her face, determined to make eye contact. "How long have you been thinking about divorcing me?"

"All the time you were with that girl."

"You knew about it before the inspector mentioned her?"

"Yes, I did!" There was a flash of anger in her eyes.

"He merely confirmed what I already knew. You must think I'm so stupid!"

"I don't." He bowed his head in shame. "I don't think you're stupid, Ellen." He looked up at her again, but she refused to meet his gaze. "Ellen, please. I realise I've been silly. I've made a mistake. But can't you forgive a silly mistake? Please believe me when I tell you she meant nothing to me. And now she's gone. We can start again! There doesn't need to be a divorce. We can forget all about it and continue as if nothing has changed. Can't you see, Ellen? Just think how much damage a divorce would do. It would have such a dreadful effect on our parents, and on our beautiful children. They would be so devastated. Won't you please reconsider?"

She turned to him at last. "How do I know that you didn't murder her?"

"Why would I do that?"

"Perhaps she threatened to reveal your affair."

"No, she didn't. And *I* didn't! Please believe me, Ellen! I can't bear this!"

Chapter 25

"Mr Evans was very happy with his copy of *A Tale of Two Cities*," Fred told Augusta in the shop the following morning.

"Mr Evans?"

"Tall man. Wears a grey coat. He came in and told me how much he'd enjoyed *Ivanhoe*."

Augusta smiled. "I know exactly who you mean now! Mr Evans is his name, is it?"

"Yes. We had quite a long chat. He told me he likes making model railways."

"That's interesting. Perhaps I should be on the lookout for books about railways. I'm pleased he bought the Dickens book. I'll have to find the time to repair some more for him."

Augusta was impressed with the way Fred had been managing in the shop over the past few days. The takings had been good and he appeared to get on well with the customers. Even the grumpy ones like Mr Evans.

"I'm sorry it's been such a busy few days," she said. "I've hardly been here, have I? Once I've finished this detective work I'll hopefully be here a lot more. I'm finding it rather difficult to fit everything in."

"I understand, Mrs Peel. I wouldn't turn down an opportunity to do a bit of private detective work myself. It sounds so exciting!"

"It can be exciting, but it can also be rather frustrating."

She paused when she saw who had just stepped in through the door. It was a man with grey hair and an impeccably tailored suit.

Thomas Bewick.

How can I pretend that I haven't found Miss Frankland-Russell now that he's right here in front of me?

"Mrs Peel!" He grinned as he glanced around the bookshop. "Isn't this a lovely place? I understand the shop is a new venture for you. Is it going well?"

"We've only been open a few weeks, Mr Bewick, but it's going well so far. Fred, my new member of staff here, has been extremely helpful."

"Oh, good. Nice to meet you, Fred! Do you mind me asking if there's somewhere we can talk privately, Mrs Peel?"

"Of course. We can speak in the room out the back."

Augusta led the way to her workshop, the lawyer following closely behind. She closed the door behind her and took a deep breath.

Thomas glanced around at the tools on the worktable and the piles of books stacked on the shelves. "So this is where you repair your books, is it? Very clever indeed. You're a talented woman, Mrs Peel."

"I wouldn't say talented, but I'm certainly very busy at the moment; particularly since I decided to take on that mysterious task you offered me."

"Yes, and that's what I'm here about. Have you found Miss Frankland-Russell yet?"

Augusta hoped her expression wouldn't betray her as she skirted his question. "I met an old friend of hers who told me Miss Frankland-Russell was working in a clothes shop on Oxford Street."

"Yes, that's what you told me the last time we met. Has there been any progress since then?"

Augusta held his gaze for a moment. "No," she said firmly.

"You haven't visited any of the shops on Oxford Street?"

"I'm in the process of visiting all the clothes shops on Oxford Street, but I'm sure you can appreciate that there are rather a lot of them. And there's always the possibility that Mrs Cooper made a mistake and it wasn't a clothes shop, but another type of shop. So really we could be talking about any of the shops on Oxford Street."

Thomas gave a slow nod, his sparkling blue eyes fixed on Augusta's face.

Does he believe me?

"I see. Perhaps you need some help with the search."

"Oh, I'll get there eventually. At least I have Fred to help me in the shop now, so I have more time to investigate." She gave a wide smile, hoping it might help to defuse the tension in the room.

It appeared to have some effect, as Thomas's face softened a little.

"It would be really helpful if you could obtain further details from Lord Frankland-Russell about the circumstances of his last communication with his daughter," she added. "Perhaps there's a possibility that she fell out with her parents and doesn't want to be found."

"I could ask him, I suppose. He didn't mention

anything like that. And, regardless of the circumstances, I'm sure he'd like to know that she's safe."

Augusta knew she somehow had to assure him that Catherine was safe and well without giving away her location. If he decided to search the shops on Oxford Street himself, it would only be a matter of time before he came across Miss Frankland-Russell. She didn't have a lot of time. "I shall carry on with my work, Mr Bewick. In fact, I'll be heading down to Oxford Street again later today. I'll let you know as soon as I have any news of her whereabouts."

"Good." He gave a broad smile. "I knew I could rely on you, Mrs Peel. I'm looking forward to hearing from you."

Augusta set to work repairing a copy of *Gulliver's Travels* as soon as Mr Bewick had left. She began by gently wiping the blue cloth cover with a piece of rubber and felt quite satisfied by the amount of grime she was able to remove using this simple technique.

Why were the three young women so reluctant to talk about each other? She felt thoroughly frustrated about the case. She was reluctant to harass Miss Frankland-Russell again, so that left Mrs Cooper to approach. It had been a couple of days since they had last spoken. *Surely it's worth another try.*

Augusta went to let Fred know that she would be heading out for an hour or so.

Chapter 26

Augusta hadn't expected to see scaffolding erected around Dorothy Cooper's house on Manchester Street. The upper storey was blackened and there were a number of workmen up on the roof, presumably carrying out repairs.

"It wasn't a large fire," explained the housekeeper when Augusta enquired about it, "but the chimney in the attic was blocked. The damage makes it look far worse than it really was."

"When did it happen?"

"Two days ago."

"The day I was last here? It must have happened not long after I left."

"Yes, it did. I'll go and tell Mrs Cooper you're here."

A few moments later, Augusta was shown into the parlour, where Dorothy was busy with her needlework at the table.

"I'm very sorry to hear about the fire, Mrs Cooper," said Augusta. "I hope no one was hurt."

"No, no one was hurt." She smiled. "I foolishly decided

to light a fire up there without giving any thought to the fact that the fireplace hadn't been used in a long while. It caused quite a bit of excitement, especially when the fire brigade arrived!"

Augusta wondered why the young woman had taken it upon herself to light a fire when she had a housekeeper to do such things on her behalf.

"How can I help you?" asked Dorothy, gesturing for Augusta to join her at the table.

"I thought you might be interested to hear that Catherine Frankland-Russell has been found safe and well."

Dorothy did not appear overjoyed at the news. Instead, she occupied herself with threading a needle. "Well, that is good news. I'm sure her parents were very relieved to hear it."

"They will be when I tell them. I wanted to thank you for being so helpful the last time we met."

"My pleasure."

Dorothy didn't appear to be in a talkative mood. Once again, Augusta felt as though she was being stonewalled. She cleared her throat and decided to tackle the subject head on.

"Now that Miss Frankland-Russell has been located, my work will focus on Miss Thackeray's murder. I hope you don't mind me saying this, Mrs Cooper, but I felt there was something you weren't telling me when we last spoke."

"What do you mean?"

"I felt as if you were holding something back."

The young woman laughed awkwardly. "Well, I wasn't."

"I felt the same way when I spoke to Miss Thackeray, and also when I spoke to Miss Frankland-Russell."

"You've spoken to Catherine?"

"Yes. I was the person who found her, thanks to you."

Dorothy rubbed her brow, then returned to her needlework.

"How did you know these two young ladies?"

"We were all friends when we were young. I'm sure I've already told you that."

"Were you at school together?"

Augusta hadn't expected Dorothy's face to stiffen in response to this simple question. She had expected her to answer it quite happily.

Instead, Dorothy looked down at her hands and hesitated before speaking. "We knew each other from school, but our families were also quite friendly with each other."

"Then you were school friends?"

"Yes, I suppose we were."

This seemed to be another odd way of answering her question. *Why can't she simply confirm that they were friends at school?*

"May I ask which school you attended?"

Dorothy took a deep breath and rolled her shoulders. "It's changed its name now. I can't honestly remember."

"You can't remember?"

"No. What's wrong with that?" Dorothy glanced up at the clock on the mantelpiece. "I need to be somewhere at twelve—"

"Of course, Mrs Cooper. I won't detain you for much longer. Where was the school?"

"Here in London."

"North? South? East? West?"

"North."

"Close to the centre or in a suburb?"

"In Hampstead," replied Dorothy with a sigh. "Is that a suburb?"

"It was a village at one time. Isn't it remarkable how

London has spread and swallowed all these places up? You seem rather reluctant to talk about your school, if you don't mind me saying so, Mrs Cooper."

"My schooldays were miserable," she said mournfully. "I don't like talking about them, nor do I like being reminded of them."

"I'm very sorry to hear that. Were Miss Thackeray and Miss Frankland-Russell equally unhappy there?"

"I can't speak for them; I can only speak for myself. And to be quite honest with you, I've pushed all my memories of that dreadful place out of my mind."

"To the point that you can't even remember the name of it?"

"It was a girls' school in Hampstead. There can't be many schools there."

"No, I don't suppose there are. Thank you, Mrs Cooper."

"What are you going to do now?" Her eyes were wide and enquiring, as if she were fearful about the consequences of sharing this information.

"I intend to find Miss Thackeray's killer."

"I don't see what the school might have to do with that."

"Neither do I. Not yet, anyway."

Chapter 27

"St Mildred's Girls' School in Hampstead," Augusta said to Philip as they walked along the river embankment that afternoon. A cold breeze blew in from the river, tugging at their overcoats. A lamplighter was lighting the lamps as dusk began to fall.

"That's the name of the school the three young women attended?" he asked.

"I'm fairly sure it could be. I've just visited Holborn Library and had a good look through the directories there. St Mildred's is a long-established school in Hampstead, but the only way to be sure it's the right one is to pay the school a visit."

"That sounds like a plan. Although confirming that the three women were at school together won't really tell us much, will it?"

"Perhaps not. But if I asked you the name of the school you went to, what would you say?"

"Watford Grammar School."

"Exactly. And I would say much the same thing."

"I don't remember ever seeing you at my school, Augusta. Besides, it's a boys' school."

She laughed. "I meant that I wouldn't hesitate to tell somebody which school I went to or where I worked."

"Unless you were working undercover in Belgium during the war."

"Well, obviously we didn't give anybody a straight answer at that time, but this is different. My point is that Dorothy Cooper claimed she couldn't remember the name of the school she attended. Don't you think that rather strange? I've never met anyone who has forgotten the name of the school they attended. It's something most people would remember."

"I agree that it does seem a little strange."

"When you couple it with the fact that none of the three women seemed keen to talk about one another, it all seems very fishy indeed. I think I need to pay the school a visit."

"To ask what?"

"I don't know yet. Perhaps just to ask for confirmation that they all went there. That would be a start."

"Sounds like a good idea."

"I received a visit from the solicitor, Thomas Bewick, this morning. He's very impatient for news of Miss Frankland-Russell's whereabouts."

"Did you tell him you had found her?"

Augusta shook her head. "I couldn't bring myself to do it. Besides, I made a promise to Catherine."

"Oh dear."

"I will tell him eventually. I just wanted to give her the opportunity to write to her parents herself."

"Do you think she'll do it?"

"I don't know. I'll have to visit her again and ask."

Philip shook his head. "You can't leave it much longer, Augusta. What if he finds out that you know?"

"How would he do that?"

"I don't know, but he might do. And then he'd be annoyed that you hadn't done the work the way he'd asked. I understand why you feel sympathy for Miss Frankland-Russell but just imagine how her parents must be feeling, with no idea where she might be."

"Her parents don't sound very pleasant."

"That's not for us to judge, Augusta. You were employed to do a job and you need to see it through."

"Thank you for the advice, Philip. Only, I'm not sure that I need it on this occasion."

"I'm only expressing my view on the matter."

"I know your view on the matter; you've already told me. Please allow me to deal with the situation the best way I see fit."

"Very well."

A steamboat chugged by, puffing out plumes of steam and smoke.

"The search for Miss Thackeray's killer is beginning to frustrate me," said Philip. "One moment I suspect Walter Mitchell and the next… I'm just not sure at all."

"What did you make of Ellen Mitchell?"

"I'm not convinced she was being entirely truthful with us. Her distraught reaction to the news of her husband's affair didn't seem very genuine to me."

"Nor me. Perhaps Mrs Mitchell murdered Miss Thackeray because she found out Miss Thackeray was having an affair with her husband."

"It's certainly a potential motive, though she claimed not to have known about the affair until I told her."

"Do you believe her?"

"I don't know. I don't see why she would lie."

"She might if she were the murderer."

"Very true. Although people often have other reasons for lying. There's certainly something odd about Mr and Mrs Mitchell, but I can't quite put my finger on it yet."

"Do you still think Miss Frankland-Russell might have carried out the murder?"

"We can't rule it out."

"I can't imagine Miss Frankland-Russell having the strength to overpower and then strangle someone."

"Perhaps it's easier to pounce on someone from behind in the dark. The murderer would have been at an advantage if he – or she – had taken Miss Thackeray by surprise."

"I just can't imagine her doing it."

"Maybe she had someone else do it for her."

"Such as? I'm quite sure she doesn't have the money to have paid someone."

"A boyfriend, perhaps? I really don't know at this stage. What I do know is that I'm getting rather frustrated with it all."

Chapter 28

AUGUSTA'S TELEPHONE rang later that evening.

"Augusta, it's Philip."

She didn't like the serious tone of his voice. "What's happened?"

"Can you get yourself over to Paddington Street Gardens in Marylebone? There's been another murder."

Augusta closed her eyes and thought for a moment.

Marylebone. Where Dorothy Cooper lives.

"It's not Mrs Cooper, is it?"

"I'm afraid so."

Augusta flagged down a taxi in Russell Square and arrived at Paddington Street Gardens fifteen minutes later.

"What's goin' on 'ere, then?" asked the cab driver, surveying the huddle of police officers. "A spot o' trouble by the looks o' things. You alright wi' me droppin' you off 'ere, miss? Don't want a lady like yerself gettin' caught up in no bother."

"I'll be fine, thank you. My friend is a detective inspector."

"Is 'e now? Yer in safe 'ands, then."

Augusta removed her torch from her handbag and walked toward the dark little park as the cab pulled away. It was shortly after ten o'clock. Despite the lateness of the hour, a small crowd of onlookers had gathered beneath the light of the lamp posts beyond the park railings. Strong gusts of wind rattled the bare branches of the trees.

Can Dorothy Cooper really be dead?

Augusta had only spoken to her earlier that day. She felt tears pricking her eyes as she thought of the young woman sitting at the parlour table with her needlework.

How could anyone have wished to harm her?

She found a constable and asked for Detective Inspector Fisher. The young chap led her through a gate in the railings to where a group of dark figures stood with their torches.

Philip's silhouette was easily identified, given that he was the only officer with a walking stick. She could just about discern his features in the dark.

"You got down here quickly, Augusta."

"This park is just like the two Bloomsbury squares," she commented, glancing up at the dark trees around them.

"No coincidence, is it?"

"Do you think it was the same attacker?"

"It's too early to be sure, but there are certainly similarities. Early indications suggest that Mrs Cooper was also strangled."

"So close to her home, too."

"Yes. This little park backs on to Manchester Street."

"Where I visited her earlier today. I still can't believe this has really happened!"

"She was found just off the path, under that tree over there. I know it's difficult to see in the dark but it's where those torchlights are. The ambulance has just departed with her body and the post-mortem will be carried out tomorrow. We'll have a little more to go on then."

"When did it happen?"

"Shortly after nightfall. Dorothy had been visiting a friend nearby and had left to return home shortly before six. She took a shortcut through this park and we've already spoken to a few people who said they heard screams. She was found by passers-by shortly after the attack. A doctor was summoned but she died before he was able to do anything to save her.

"Let's hope we'll be able to find more witnesses. There must be someone who saw the culprit running away from the park. There are plenty of houses around and the road is quite a busy one. I can't begin to fathom how someone had the gall to commit an act like that in the early evening. It was obviously someone who felt very determined and sure of himself."

"Someone who had perhaps been following Mrs Cooper or knew that she would be walking this way?" suggested Augusta. "It's unlikely to have been a random attack, isn't it? The similarities to Miss Thackeray's murder are too great."

"They are. This shouldn't have happened. We should have arrested the murderer before he got to Mrs Cooper."

"There's no chance that Mrs Cooper's husband could have attacked her, is there?"

"There's certainly a chance. D Division are speaking to him at the moment. I'll interview him myself as well, but I'm more inclined to think it was the same person who attacked Miss Thackeray."

"First Miss Thackeray and now Mrs Cooper," mused Augusta. "Did someone want to silence them? It's no accident that these murders have coincided with my search for Miss Frankland-Russell, is it?" Her stomach turned at the thought. "I feel responsible for their deaths."

"You're not responsible, Augusta."

"But it's too much of a coincidence that they should occur at this point in time. The connection between the two murders *has* to be Miss Frankland-Russell. I wish I hadn't begun asking questions now."

"You mustn't blame yourself."

"It's hard not to. It was only today that I last spoke to Mrs Cooper! Was someone watching us? Did she tell me something she shouldn't have? All I got was the name of the school. Why would that be so significant? Dorothy didn't want to tell me the name of the school, but I pushed her until I was able to work it out."

"The link could be Miss Frankland-Russell," said Philip, "but none of this is your fault, Augusta. We don't fully understand the motives for Miss Thackeray and Mrs Cooper's deaths yet. Until we know that, it's all speculation. Hopefully the killer has left us a clue this time. We may get a better idea of what happened when we return to the park in daylight, speak to more witnesses and find out the results of the post-mortem."

Augusta shivered. "It's barbaric," she said. "What if he doesn't stop at two murders? Who's next on his list?"

"No one, hopefully. I sincerely hope that we'll get him before anyone else can be harmed." A police officer approached them. "Yes, Sergeant Stevens?" said Philip. "It is Stevens, isn't it? It's tricky to tell in the dark."

"Yes, sir. I just thought I'd let you know that we've received some interesting information from the neighbours.

Several have reported that Mrs Cooper had a visitor this afternoon."

"Who was it?"

"We don't know yet. But we do know that he was riding a motorcycle with a sidecar."

Chapter 29

"WE DON'T ALLOW civilians to participate in interviews as a general rule," said Inspector Shellbrook at Marylebone Lane police station the following morning.

"Can you make an allowance on this occasion?" asked Philip. "Mrs Peel is a private detective and has been assisting me with the investigation into Elizabeth Thackeray's murder."

Augusta watched Inspector Shellbrook's thick moustache bristling as he gave this some thought. "As a rule," he replied, "we don't allow it."

Philip eventually managed to persuade the inspector from D Division to bend the rules and Augusta seated herself in the small interview room with a notebook. She was permitted to be there on the condition that she said nothing throughout the interview.

It wasn't long before Walter Mitchell was brought in. His clothes were creased and his boyish face suddenly looked older, with shadows beneath his eyes and rough stubble on his chin.

"I don't understand what I'm doing here," he said as

he sat himself down on one of the uncomfortable wooden chairs. "I didn't even know Dorothy Cooper." Then his eyes fell on Augusta. "You!" he said, accusingly. "You were the woman who spoke to Elizabeth. I saw you at the school. Who *are* you? And what are you doing here?"

Inspector Shellbrook rolled his eyes and looked pointedly at Philip, as if to suggest that Augusta's presence was already proving to be a disruption.

Philip explained why Augusta was there and followed up with his first question. "Why did you visit Dorothy Cooper yesterday afternoon?"

"I wanted to find out what Elizabeth had spoken to her about."

Philip put on his reading glasses and consulted his papers. "Miss Thackeray visited Mrs Cooper five days ago. Why did you wait until yesterday to ask her?"

"I suppose I'd only just thought of it. I felt so incredibly helpless, so I decided to carry out some investigations of my own. I'm no good at it, of course, but I felt the need to do something. I wouldn't have had to if you lot had already caught the man!"

"Did Mrs Cooper have anything useful to tell you?"

"No, she didn't. I don't think she wanted me there."

"What did you ask her?"

"I asked why Elizabeth had visited her. I mentioned that she had decided to do so after that lady over there—" He pointed at Augusta.

"Mrs Peel."

"After Mrs Peel had spoken to her."

"Two young women have been murdered within the space of a week, Mr Mitchell," commented Philip, "and we happen to know that you saw both of them shortly before their deaths."

"That's just a coincidence, Inspector! I really don't

know how to convince you of that, but I'm just as horrified by all this as you are."

"And neither Mrs Cooper nor Miss Thackeray told you what their conversation that day was about?"

"No! That's why I wanted to speak to Mrs Cooper, but now she's dead, too. I know what it looks like, but I had nothing to do with it!"

"We suspect there must have been a secret between them that neither wished to divulge," said Philip. "We believe both young women were targeted for a reason. Do you have any idea what the secret might have been?"

Walter paused and ran a hand through his scruffy hair. Augusta sensed there was something he wanted to tell them but, just as she was starting to feel hopeful, he leaned forward on the table and fixed his gaze on Philip. "I've got nothing to say. I know nothing of any secrets."

"What time did you visit Mrs Cooper?" asked Inspector Shellbrook.

"About four o'clock. I'm normally teaching at that time, but my students were at the National Gallery yesterday. We're lucky to have so many excellent art galleries close by for them to visit. Anyway, it meant that I had time to visit Mrs Cooper."

"How long did you stay?"

"Not long. Five or ten minutes."

"And then where did you go?"

"I went for a drive to clear my head."

"Why?"

"I felt frustrated because Mrs Cooper wouldn't tell me why Elizabeth had visited her. I didn't know what to do next."

"Did you return to Manchester Street later on?"

"No. Why would I do that? Mrs Cooper had made it quite clear that she didn't want to speak to me."

"What were her exact words to you?"

He scratched at his scalp. "I can't remember her exact words, but it was something along the lines of, 'Elizabeth and I had a brief and private conversation that I have no wish to discuss with anyone else.'"

"Did she mention the fire at her home?" asked Inspector Shellbrook.

"No. I saw that there was some repair work going on, but she didn't mention it."

"A conversation with her housekeeper revealed that the fire started when Mrs Cooper tried to burn some personal papers in the fireplace of an attic room."

Augusta listened closely to this. Although she had known about the fire, she wasn't aware that Mrs Cooper had been burning personal papers. Augusta knew she had been forbidden to speak, but she couldn't help herself. "The fire occurred shortly after I visited Mrs Cooper and asked her about Miss Thackeray," she said. "Having just learned that she was burning personal papers, I'm beginning to wonder whether she did so in response to my visit."

"Very interesting!" exclaimed Walter. "Have you thought about arresting Mrs Peel here? She also visited Elizabeth and Mrs Cooper shortly before they were murdered. Surely she's a suspect, too?"

Augusta said nothing, aware that her words had caused a further interruption to the interview.

"No woman could have inflicted such severe injuries on Mrs Cooper," said Inspector Shellbrook. "And while I can't speak for the murder of Miss Thackeray, because it didn't take place under my jurisdiction, I suspect that the same is true in that case, too. Let's not get distracted here. Not a word more from you, please, Mrs Peel."

"You're wasting your time interviewing me when you could be out there looking for the man who did this," said

Walter. "This is the second time I've been forced to answer for myself! Can't you just let me go home to my wife? The most important thing for me to do now is rescue my marriage. You do realise, don't you, Detective Inspector Fisher, that you have caused a great deal of damage by revealing the affair to my wife?"

"I do apologise, Mr Mitchell. We have to question people on a range of matters and sometimes that involves digging up unpleasant truths, I'm afraid. How is your wife?"

"She wants to divorce me."

"Oh, I'm very sorry to hear it. I hope that's not due to the news I had to share with her."

"No. It turns out she'd been considering it for a while. She knew about the affair, you see, but she never confronted me about it. Instead, she began plotting with a solicitor behind my back, and now she intends to petition for divorce. I'm trying to persuade her otherwise. Can't you see that my life is difficult enough as it is without you dragging me in here and asking me even more questions?"

Ellen Mitchell lied, thought Augusta. *She knew about her husband's affair with Elizabeth Thackeray all along.* She watched Philip closely, wondering if he would impart this information to Walter.

"I have no further questions for Mr Mitchell, Inspector Shellbrook," Philip said impassively. "Do you?"

"No. Nothing more from me at the moment."

"Thank you, Mr Mitchell," said Philip. "You're free to go."

Chapter 30

Augusta and Philip made the short walk from Marylebone Lane to Stanhope Fashions on Oxford Street. The brisk wind from the previous day had dropped and the streets were bathed in weak, early-winter sunlight.

"According to Mr Mitchell, his wife knew about the affair with Miss Thackeray before I told her," said Philip. "We need to have a good explanation from her for why she felt the need to lie to me about that."

Augusta spotted the bespectacled shop girl, Barbara, as soon they stepped inside. She didn't recognise the other girl, and there was no obvious sign of Miss Frankland-Russell or Mrs Mitchell.

"Mrs Mitchell is at a meeting with her lawyer," replied Barbara when Philip asked for her with a flash of his warrant card.

"Do you happen to know who her lawyer is and where his office might be?"

"No, but perhaps the details can be found in her office." She led them into a small, tidy office at the back of the shop. A large appointments diary rested on the desk and Barbara opened it. "'Mr Bewick, ten o'clock'," she read out. "It doesn't actually say where his office is."

"*Thomas* Bewick?" asked Philip.

"I don't know."

"We'll make an educated guess that it's him. Thank you, Barbara. You've been very helpful."

"Is Lucy in today?" Augusta asked.

Barbara shook her head. "She was supposed to be in, but she hasn't turned up. I don't know where she is."

"Mr *Bewick*?" Augusta said to Philip as they left the shop. "Can we be sure that it's the Mr Bewick we know?"

"There's only one way to find out. His office is very near here, isn't it? In Cavendish Square? There's no harm in checking it out."

They turned into Holles Street and made their way up to the square.

"I wonder where Miss Frankland-Russell has got to," commented Augusta. "I hope she hasn't run off again. Perhaps she didn't believe me when I promised not to tell her parents where she was."

"Perhaps. Wasn't she supposed to be writing them a letter?"

"I encouraged her to do so. But whether she will or not, I really couldn't say."

On their arrival, Thomas Bewick's fashionable young secretary informed the pair that the lawyer was busy.

"Yes, we thought he might be," replied Philip. "Is he in a meeting with Ellen Mitchell?"

The young woman fidgeted with her hands. "His clients' names are confidential, I'm afraid."

"I'm sure they are. However, I'm an inspector from Scotland Yard, and I'd really like to speak to Mrs Mitchell as soon as possible." He showed the secretary his warrant card.

"I'm not supposed to disturb Mr Bewick when he's with a client."

"I'm afraid you must when an inspector from Scotland Yard requests it."

She sniffed and walked off toward Mr Bewick's office.

"I suppose there's always a chance that it's a different Mr Bewick she's meeting with," Philip whispered to Augusta. "We'd look rather foolish then, wouldn't we? It's important that we at least pretend to know exactly what we're doing, though."

The secretary returned a short while later and said that Mr Bewick was willing to admit them.

If Thomas Bewick was irritated by the interruption, he didn't show it. "This is a surprise, Inspector. Has something happened?" Dressed in a smart grey suit with a burgundy tie and handkerchief, he leaned against his desk as he spoke.

Ellen Mitchell was dressed in blue and sat scowling at them from one of the plum-coloured sofas.

"Something or other is always happening, Mr Bewick," replied Philip. "I do apologise for the interruption, but we would really appreciate a quick word with Mrs Mitchell, if it's not too inconvenient. It won't take long."

"Of course. I'll pop downstairs while you do that."

"No, wait!" Ellen called out. "I'd like you to stay here, Mr Bewick." She turned to Philip. "Anything you have to say to me can be said in the presence of my lawyer."

Philip glanced at Thomas, who gave an acquiescent nod. "Very well," he said.

Augusta and Philip took a seat on the sofa opposite Ellen, who was immediately joined by her lawyer.

"We've got a bit of a conundrum on our hands, Mrs Mitchell," said Philip. "We spoke to your husband this morning, and one thing he said contradicted something you told us."

"That doesn't surprise me at all," she replied. "You've hauled him in for questioning again, have you? I imagine he's extremely tired and disorientated by now. It's no wonder he's started contradicting himself."

"He's not contradicting *himself*, Mrs Mitchell. He's contradicting *you*."

"He recently discovered that I intend to divorce him, Inspector, so his mind is probably very muddled. If you must know, that was the reason for my visit to Mr Bewick this morning."

"I see. I'm sorry to hear about the divorce. I realise this must be a difficult time for you, so I'll get on with it. Why did you pretend not to know about your husband's affair?"

Ellen pushed her lower lip out and gave a bemused shrug. "Are you accusing me of lying, Inspector?"

"It seems you knew about the affair with Elizabeth Thackeray before I told you about it. Is that right?"

Ellen glanced across at her lawyer, then back at Philip. "I knew he was up to something. A wife always knows."

"But did you know it was Elizabeth Thackeray he was having an affair with?"

She smoothed her hair, then examined a manicured fingernail. "I saw them together once. She was in his sidecar. We don't live very far from the university, you see."

"So you're now admitting that you knew your husband

148

was having an affair with Miss Thackeray before I shared that information with you?"

She scratched behind her ear. "I had an inkling. Is that all you need to know? Mr Bewick and I have a lot of work to be getting on with."

"May I ask why you lied to us, Mrs Mitchell?"

"I don't recall lying to you."

"When I informed you of your husband's *friendship*, as I put it, with Mrs Thackeray, you acted as though it were a shocking piece of news to you."

"I don't recall that, but I remember being quite upset. It always upsets me to hear any mention of it." She pulled a handkerchief from her handbag and dabbed at her face with it, unconvincingly.

"Is there anything else, Inspector?" asked Mr Bewick.

"Just one more question. Mrs Mitchell, did you know about your husband's relationship with Elizabeth Thackeray before she was murdered?"

"How would I remember that? I know that I found out quite recently, but I can't even remember when the girl was murdered now."

"It was five days ago. Were you aware of the affair before then?"

"I'd say that it was quite likely, yes. I think I was already speaking to Mr Bewick by that point."

"Let me consult my notes," Thomas said, getting up from his seat. He strode over to the large desk and leafed through some papers. "I can confirm that Mrs Mitchell first called on me exactly six days ago. It was then that she first asked me about obtaining a divorce."

"The day before Elizabeth Thackeray was murdered," replied Philip.

"But looking back at my notes," continued the lawyer, "I see that there is no mention of Mr Mitchell's affair or of the girl, so I'm unable to confirm whether my client knew of the affair when she visited my office."

Augusta was disappointed to hear this. Mr Bewick seemed to be providing Mrs Mitchell with a reasonable defence.

Philip turned to Ellen. "But surely you can recall whether you knew about your husband's affair or not at that point?"

"My memory is rather vague now," she responded. "Our marriage hasn't been right for a long time."

"I don't like being lied to, Mrs Mitchell."

"To the best of my recollection, I have never actually lied to you, Inspector. Didn't you just deduce that my husband's affair with Elizabeth Thackeray was news to me the last time we spoke?"

Philip ran his hand over his chin, clearly frustrated that she was deliberately complicating the matter. He rose to his feet and picked up his walking stick.

"Thank you for your time, Mrs Mitchell. Mr Bewick."

He began to walk toward the door, and Augusta followed behind him.

"If there's anything else I can help with, Inspector, please don't hesitate to call on me again," said Thomas Bewick. "Oh, and Mrs Peel?"

Augusta reluctantly turned to face him, knowing what he was about to ask.

"Any word on the matter we recently discussed?"

"I'm afraid not, Mr Bewick. I really don't know where she is."

"She's lying, isn't she?" said Philip as they stepped out onto Cavendish Square. "In fact, she's lying about lying! How irritating that we decided to speak to her without all the relevant documents in front of us. It was a bit rash going to see her at her solicitor's office. I'll head back to the Yard to go through the file and reread her exact words from that interview."

"She's very cunning," added Augusta. "I hope you manage to find something helpful in the notes. I wonder why she's lying to us?"

"That's anyone's guess. I suppose you'll need to be getting back to the shop now."

"I really should, but I'll have to trust Fred to mind things a short while longer. I'd like to pay a visit to St Mildred's School in Hampstead first."

Chapter 31

ST MILDRED'S SCHOOL FOR GIRLS was a large, austere, red-brick building with mullioned windows. It sat within modest-sized grounds close to a wealthy residential area in South Hampstead. It was easy to reach by tube, and the faint warmth of the sun made the walk along its gravelled driveway quite pleasant.

A neat sign at the entrance door informed Augusta that the headmistress's name was Miss Roberts. Once inside, she was informed by Miss Roberts's secretary that the headmistress would only be able to see her for ten minutes.

Moments later, Augusta found herself standing inside a large office. One wall was lined with books while another had tall, leaded windows that looked out over the grounds. Portraits of various stern-faced women hung on the walls. Augusta deduced that they depicted former teachers and notable alumni.

As she seated herself opposite Miss Roberts, Augusta felt fidgety and light-headed. This situation reminded her of being scolded by the headmistress during her own schooldays. She tried to reassure herself that those days had long since passed.

Miss Roberts was about fifty years old with wavy grey hair and horn-rimmed spectacles. A neat bow had been tied at the collar of her dark-blue blouse.

"I'm a private detective," Augusta explained, "and I'm assisting Scotland Yard with one of their investigations. You've no doubt heard about the recent deaths of two young women: Elizabeth Thackeray and Dorothy Cooper. Mrs Cooper's maiden name was Henderson. I understand both girls attended this school."

"Yes, I believe they did," replied the headmistress solemnly. "I wasn't here during their time but I heard from members of my staff that the two women studied here. It's caused a great deal of shock, as I'm sure you can imagine; to the teachers who knew them and also to the school as a whole. It's dreadful to think that something so awful could happen to two former pupils."

"Miss Thackeray and Mrs Cooper had a friend, Catherine Frankland-Russell. I understand she was also a pupil here."

"Was she? I couldn't tell you, I'm afraid."

"Is there a teacher I can speak to who might remember Miss Frankland-Russell? And the other two girls as well?"

Miss Roberts glanced up at the clock on the mantelpiece. "Lessons will be finishing shortly. Miss Worsley might see you, I suppose. She's the games mistress and has been teaching here for about fifteen years. She might remember the girls."

Augusta followed Miss Roberts as she walked briskly along the corridor, the tap-tap of her heels echoing noisily on the wooden floorboards. She pushed open a door that opened out onto a colonnaded walkway. Beyond this lay a large emerald-green playing field where a game of lacrosse was in progress. Miss Roberts strode out onto the field and Augusta trailed after her.

As she approached the girls, she recalled being hit in the face by a lacrosse ball at her own school. She had lost a tooth in the incident but had been instructed to play on regardless. She resolved not to hold Miss Worsley in the same contempt in which she had held her own games mistress all those years ago.

The whistle sounded and the girls immediately stopped playing. Miss Worsley gave the girls who hadn't put in enough effort a dressing-down, then dispatched everyone back to the changing rooms.

"Miss Worsley," said the headmistress, "this is Mrs Peel, a private detective. She has some questions about Elizabeth Thackeray and Dorothy Cooper, or Dorothy Henderson, as she was known during her time here. You remember them, don't you?"

"I do."

Miss Worsley was a broad-shouldered woman of about forty. She wore a navy blazer and skirt with a matching headband to keep her bobbed hair in place.

"Do you remember a friend of theirs, Catherine Frankland-Russell?" asked Augusta.

"Yes, I remember her all right." She appeared to have no fond memories of the girl, judging by her solemn expression.

"Would you mind telling me exactly what you remember of them?" Augusta asked. "I spoke to both Elizabeth Thackeray and Dorothy Cooper before they were killed, but they were reluctant to say much about each other. I've found Catherine Frankland-Russell to be equally reluctant. It's as if they've all been tasked with keeping some sort of secret. I'm beginning to believe that the secret must be uncovered if the murders are ever to be solved."

Miss Worsley fixed her gaze on the houses at the far end of the playing field. "I'm guessing that will have something to do with Mrs McCall," she responded.

Augusta heard an intake of breath from the headmistress next to her.

"Who's Mrs McCall?" Augusta asked.

The games mistress turned to face Miss Roberts and, raising one hand to shield her eyes from the low sun, asked, "am I permitted to explain?"

"In the briefest of words," responded the headmistress. "It's a matter we prefer not to discuss here at St Mildred's."

"It happened during the war," Miss Worsley told Augusta. "In early 1915. That was when Mrs McCall died."

"How dreadful. It was quite sudden, was it?"

"I'd say so. She fell down the main staircase."

"She died here at the school?"

"Unfortunately, yes. Shortly before she died, she'd been involved in an altercation with a group of girls. Troublemakers, they were."

"Elizabeth, Dorothy and Catherine?"

"Yes, and two more. Susan Peterson and Mary Colbourne."

"And she fell because of the altercation?"

"Well, that's the trouble. No one really knows for sure."

"I hope this has answered your question, Mrs Peel," interrupted the headmistress, "but it's obviously not an incident we are keen to dwell on."

"It's very shocking," replied Augusta. "Were the police involved?"

"They were," responded Miss Worsley, "and if you ask me, they struggled to manage those five girls or get anything pertinent out of them. They played the police like a fiddle. Ridiculous, isn't it? The police can catch all manner of crooks and gangsters, but a group of school-girls? They just didn't know what to do with them. They let them all go in the end. The girls protected each other, and that was that."

"That really is all we have time for," interjected Miss Roberts. "I'm sorry to hurry you, Mrs Peel, but Miss Worsley has another class to teach."

Chapter 32

"HERE ARE THE FILES," said Philip, walking into his office with a heavy box under his arm.

Augusta had called in at Scotland Yard following her visit to St Mildred's and was relieved to discover that he hadn't yet left for home.

"Let me take that box from you," she said, worried he was about to topple over as he tried to balance with his walking stick.

She placed the box down on his desk and Philip opened it. He pulled out a file and read the details on the first page. "January 1915," he announced. "Does that sound about right?"

Augusta nodded.

He pulled out another file and handed it to her. Then the pair sat down to read about the circumstances of Anne McCall's death.

Between them, they deduced that the teacher had been admitted to hospital on the 12th of January 1915, having suffered serious injuries from a fall down the staircase at Saint Mildred's. She had died from her injuries later that evening. Shortly before her accident, there had been a disagreement between her and a group of five girls: Elizabeth Thackeray, Catherine Frankland-Russell, Dorothy Henderson, Susan Peterson and Mary Colbourne. The girls were aged fifteen and sixteen at the time.

The incident appeared to have followed a series of disagreements between these girls and the schoolmistress. Dorothy Henderson had felt picked on by Mrs McCall and had been angry to have received what she believed to be excessive punishments for minor misdemeanours. The case file suggested that she had been successful in rallying support from her friends and in confronting the teacher. Following the incident, all of the girls had been expelled.

"There's a lot to read through here," said Philip. "From what I can see, there are numerous statements relating to the bickering and tension that led up to Mrs McCall's death. There are statements here from each of the girls and it appears that it wasn't just Dorothy who felt picked on. Each had a tale to tell about constant punishments such as being made to stand outside for long periods, being hit on the hands and legs with a cane, and being made to translate lengthy passages of the Greek New Testament. Not unusual punishments in themselves, but the fact that they were handed out for little or no wrongdoing seems to be the thing that angered the girls.

"Some of them told their parents about it and Dorothy Henderson's parents wrote to the headmistress. That letter has been added to this file. Mrs McCall is reported to have been angry that Dorothy's parents complained and she bore a particular grudge against the girl after that." He continued to flick through the documents in front of him.

"The headmistress at the time doesn't appear to have handled the situation well," said Augusta. "It says here that her name was Mrs Jones."

"No, it doesn't appear to have been handled well at all," agreed Philip. "And this sorry series of events culminated in a slanging match at the top of the stairs that day in January 1915. The girls said that the schoolmistress fell by accident, but the school and the police believed she was pushed."

"Why did they think that?"

"The girls' statements didn't match up. Some said Mrs McCall had stumbled and fallen down the stairs of her own accord. Others said Mrs McCall had given one of the girls a shove and that the girl had reciprocated."

"They said that she pushed Mrs McCall down the stairs?"

"It seems that way."

"Which girl was it?"

"No one was ever named," replied Philip. "They must have agreed between themselves not to drop anyone in it. I can see now that it must have been a difficult case to investigate. The only witnesses were the five girls, and they were all treated as suspects. It's no wonder they all tried to cover for themselves."

"And each other. I wonder where Susan Peterson and Mary Colbourne are now."

"It would be interesting to track them down and find out if they'd be willing to speak about the sorry event all these years later. I'll get someone to search them out. I imagine a dark cloud lingered over the girls and their friendships after they were expelled."

"I can see now why they didn't like to talk about it."

"I should think it was an episode they were all extremely ashamed about. If only we'd known this sooner, we could have asked Miss Thackeray and Mrs Cooper about it."

Augusta recalled the fire at Dorothy Cooper's home.

"Didn't the housekeeper say that Mrs Cooper had been burning personal papers? I wonder if they contained any references to the school? Perhaps she was trying to eliminate any record that could tie her to it or to Mrs McCall's death."

"She may well have been trying to do that."

"Could one of the five girls be a murderer?"

"It's possible, isn't it? If Anne McCall was pushed, the girl who did it probably didn't have murder in mind prior to the event. It's likely that she intended to inflict a great deal of harm upon her, though."

"It makes me wonder whether the motive for Miss Thackeray and Mrs Cooper's murders was revenge," said Augusta.

"And if the murderer was seeking revenge on behalf of Mrs McCall, Miss Frankland-Russell may also be in danger."

"She wasn't at the shop today," said Augusta, feeling a growing sense of alarm. "We need to find her!"

"Do you happen to know where she lives?"

"No."

"I've a bad feeling about this, Augusta. I'm going to alert Marylebone and Holborn divisions right away. I fear we may have another attack to investigate very shortly."

Philip picked up the receiver and made a couple of telephone calls. While he spoke to his colleagues, Augusta continued to read through the files.

She stopped when she heard a note of bitter disappointment in his voice. "What's wrong?" she asked, looking up.

He sighed and wiped a hand over his face. "There's no need for us to go looking for Catherine Frankland-Russell," he replied. "We're too late."

Chapter 33

"SHE'S BEEN TAKEN to University College Hospital," said Philip.

"She's still alive?"

He nodded. "It sounded as though she were dead at first, but it turns out she's just badly injured. The poor girl! Hopefully she'll make a full recovery. Let's go and talk to her. We desperately need to stop whoever's doing this."

As they travelled to the hospital by taxi, Philip related the facts of the case to Augusta. "According to the sergeant at Holborn station, the attack happened yesterday evening, shortly after nightfall. Miss Frankland-Russell – or Lucy Briggs, as she's been calling herself – was walking home from work and had just crossed Euston Road. She was attacked close to her lodgings in Longford Street. She was walking along Osnaburgh Street, by the church. It's pretty much opposite Great Portland Street tube station, so it would have been busy. The attack was foiled by passers-by who rushed over to help. He ran away before anyone could stop him. It seems our assailant is getting desperate. He decided to attack in a much busier location this time."

"How horrible."

"Visiting time is over," said the stern-faced nurse on the ward where Catherine was being treated.

"We'll be very quick," replied Philip, showing her his warrant card.

"It doesn't matter how quick you are, Inspector. It's half-past eight, so it's too late to be visiting her today."

"Lucy Briggs was attacked by a very dangerous man, Nurse. We suspect this was the third time he's done such a thing. You are aware that two young women were recently murdered, are you not? It's becoming increasingly difficult to reassure the people of London that they are safe while this man is on the loose. We need to speak to Miss Briggs and get a good description of him. I want our officers combing the streets for the culprit immediately."

The nurse sighed. "No more than five minutes, then. Miss Briggs is very tired and she's had an awful shock. Bed number eighteen."

Augusta and Philip made their way through the long ward which reeked of disinfectant. Their footsteps echoed noisily on the linoleum floor. Augusta attempted to tread carefully, many of the patients were either resting or asleep.

"I'm glad you're here with me, Augusta," whispered Philip. "You're a useful chaperone. I don't think these ladies would have cared to see a man striding through here otherwise."

Bed eighteen was at the far end of the ward. Catherine smiled weakly when she saw Augusta. Her unusually pale face contrasted with her dark hair, and there was bruising on her cheek and around her throat.

"How are you, Miss Frankland-Russell?" asked Augusta.

"Relieved to still be alive," Catherine replied. "I should have known I'd be next."

"Why didn't you tell us about Mrs McCall?"

Catherine turned away. "There wasn't really anything to say about it."

"But at least we would have had a plausible motive for the attacks on Miss Thackeray and Mrs Cooper if you had."

Catherine turned back to face her. "Even if you'd known the reason, you wouldn't have been able to stop him."

"We need to catch him," said Philip. He sat down in a chair and rested his walking stick against the bed before pulling out a notebook and pen. "Now, what did he look like?"

"I didn't really see because he came up behind me. He was wearing a rough coat... possibly tweed, because it felt scratchy against my neck and face."

"You didn't see anything of him at all?"

"No. It was dark and it all happened too quickly for me to react. He pushed me over, then I felt something around my neck. A bit of rope. I managed to cry out before he pulled it tight and that's when the people walking nearby heard me. It was terrifying. I couldn't breathe!" Her eyes grew watery. "I was so relieved when they stopped him. I'd like to thank them, but I don't know who they were."

"You've had a lucky escape," said Philip. "It was fortunate that there were people close by and they were very brave to run to your aid like that. Before we move on, is there anything else you can tell me about the man who attacked you? Did he speak at all?"

"He said, 'This is for Annie!' And then I felt the rope around my neck."

"How did his voice sound?"

"Normal."

"There was no accent that you could detect?"

"No."

"The name Annie. I assume he was referring to Anne McCall. Do you think the attack was carried out as an act of vengeance for her death?"

"I suppose so. I didn't register who he meant at the time. It wasn't until afterwards that I made the connection."

"Mrs McCall's husband, perhaps?"

"I don't know."

"Did you ever meet her husband?"

"No."

"What can you tell us about Mrs McCall's death?" Philip asked. "Was she pushed?"

Catherine turned away again. "She tripped and fell."

"No one pushed her?"

"No."

"Mrs Peel and I have just been reading the statements made by you and your friends at the time," said Philip. "Several people stated that she was pushed."

"She wasn't."

"Did she push you or one of your friends first?"

"No." The young woman screwed her eyes up. "I don't want to talk about this all over again. It was bad enough when it first happened!"

A nurse overheard Catherine's distressed voice from further down the ward and began striding towards them.

"All right," replied Philip. "Just one more question for now, then we'll leave you be. Do you happen to know the current whereabouts of Susan Peterson or Mary Colbourne?"

"I don't know about Susan, but I heard that Mary died a few years ago."

"Really?" queried Philip. "Do you know what the cause of death was?"

"She was found in the River Thames. I don't know how it happened."

The nurse reached them. "Miss Briggs needs to rest now, Inspector. She's been through a dreadful ordeal."

"Of course."

They bid Catherine goodnight and the nurse escorted them out of the ward.

"Miss Briggs must not leave this hospital without having somewhere safe to go," Philip told the nurse. "Can the ward be locked at night?"

"Why would it need to be locked?"

"It just does. Don't let anyone in unless you can be sure that they are who they say they are. I'll arrange for a constable to be stationed here."

The nurse's eyes grew wide. "Is Miss Briggs in danger?"

"Yes, she may well be."

Chapter 34

"Mr Evans has been asking for more books by Charles Dickens," said Fred in the bookshop the following day.

"He's already finished *A Tale of Two Cities*?"

"Apparently so."

Augusta sighed. "If only I'd had time to repair the copy of *Little Dorrit* sitting in the workshop. There's a copy of *Nicolas Nickleby* in there, too. Would you mind asking which he'd prefer to read when he next pops in?"

"I will, although *Nicholas Nickleby* definitely gets my vote."

"See if you can persuade him to choose that one, then. It's not quite as damaged as *Little Dorrit* and may be quicker to repair. Thank you for your help, Fred. I don't know what I'd have done without you this past week."

"I'm enjoying it. It's a good location, isn't it? There are always people passing by, and I've found that rearranging the window display each day generates new interest. That's something I always liked to do at Webster's."

"I think it's an excellent idea and, judging by our recent takings, it's an effective one too. It gives me peace of mind to know that I can trust you with the place. The case I'm working on will hopefully be solved soon and then I'll have more time to dedicate to my bookshop. I've also been a bit remiss about visiting an old friend of mine. Sparky's owner, as it happens. I'm looking after him for Lady Hereford while she's in hospital."

"Will she want him back when she comes out?"

"Yes, I suspect she will. It'll be a sad day when Sparky returns to her, but I know they'll be happy together." Augusta felt a heaviness in her heart at the thought of his departure. "I'll close the shop for an hour at lunchtime," she continued. "That way, I can visit Lady Hereford and you can have a well-deserved break."

"An hour seems rather long, Mrs Peel. I don't want us to lose out on any custom. Ten minutes will be plenty of time for me to pop out and get a sandwich."

"Really? But you need a break, Fred!"

"I'll be fine. It's a habit of mine to keep working steadily through the day."

"Well, only if you're sure."

"Oh, I'm quite sure!"

"It sounds as though Catherine Frankland-Russell is lucky to be alive," said Lady Hereford, looking up from the newspaper in her hospital bed.

Augusta started. "How do you know it was Catherine Frankland-Russell who was attacked?"

"It names her here. Though, apparently, she was using the name Lucy Briggs. Isn't she the one you were looking for?"

"Yes, and I found her. But she didn't want her parents to find out where she was." Augusta felt an uncomfortable twinge in her stomach. "Now they'll almost certainly find out."

"What's wrong with that?"

"Her parents were trying to force her to marry Hugh Farrell."

Lady Hereford lowered her newspaper once again. "That's right, they were! I remember now. That was the connection he had with the family. I couldn't remember the exact details when I suggested his name to you. How did you get on with him, by the way? I hope Detective Inspector Fisher accompanied you there."

"He didn't, because I'd already visited Mr Farrell before he had the chance to offer. Let's just say that Mr Farrell ended up with a hot cup of tea in his lap."

Lady Hereford laughed. "Oh dear, I do apologise. He's an awful man, isn't he? No wonder Catherine ran away."

Augusta updated Lady Hereford on the case. Bored of sitting about in the hospital, the old lady always liked to hear all the latest news.

"The important thing now is that Catherine is kept safe," said Augusta.

"Shouldn't she be made to stand trial for the murder of that poor teacher?"

"It would be really helpful if she could just be honest about what happened."

"It would indeed. There must be some sort of punishment in place for lying to the police. Justice hasn't been done."

"I don't know if she lied, exactly. She just hasn't been terribly forthcoming with the truth."

"You're defending her, Augusta. I don't see what possible defence there can be for such actions!"

"Perhaps the girls' youthfulness at the time should be taken into account."

"How old were they back then? Fifteen? Sixteen? Old enough to know better, I would say. I think Catherine and the other one who hasn't died yet should stand trial."

"That's for the police to decide, Lady Hereford."

"I'm not saying the other girls deserved to be murdered. No one deserves that. But you can't blame someone for coming after them if they were all involved in killing that poor teacher or covering it up. What an awful thing to do! And in a school, of all places. I suspect she was only trying to do her job. Young girls today never like being told what to do, that's the problem. Insubordination of that sort would never have been tolerated in my day. Nor yours, Augusta. I don't know what sort of a generation we're rearing these days."

"Catherine isn't safe. She needs to be protected."

"But if she played a part in her teacher's death, she should be held to account. And if she didn't, I suppose the safest place would be her parents' home. They're up in Shropshire, aren't they? That's right, Harkup House. Far away from this madman who's going around murdering everybody involved in that teacher's death."

"I imagine the parents will have found out where their daughter is by now," said Augusta. "And I've just realised that someone else will also know."

She felt a sudden sense of dread as it dawned on her that Thomas Bewick would also have discovered where Miss Frankland-Russell was, despite the fact that Augusta hadn't yet informed him.

Chapter 35

Augusta's telephone rang not long after she had returned home from the hospital that evening.

"Mrs Peel?" said the voice. "It's Thomas Bewick here."

Augusta grimaced. He had already caught up with her. "Good evening, Mr Bewick," she said cheerily. "How may I help?"

"I take it you read about the recent attack on Miss Frankland-Russell in the newspapers?"

"Yes, I did."

"Did you know where Miss Frankland-Russell was before the reports were published?" he asked.

Augusta didn't want to lie to the lawyer; she was hopeless at lying. She decided it was probably best to explain herself, but chose her words carefully. "I must admit that I did, Mr Bewick. I had a very good reason for not telling you immediately, however, and please don't think for a moment that I wasn't planning to tell you at all."

"You're telling me that her poor parents had to wait until today to find out where she was, yet you knew several days ago?"

"Yes, I had already found her, but she swore me to secrecy. She told me her parents wanted her to marry an extremely unpleasant man named Hugh Farrell. I felt rather a lot of sympathy for her predicament and said that I would keep her whereabouts quiet for a few days providing that she wrote to her parents to inform them she was safe and well."

"What you're saying, Mrs Peel, is that you didn't tell me because you believed Miss Frankland-Russell's side of the story."

"Yes."

"I'm quite sure that Lord Frankland-Russell would have given his side of the story if we had asked him."

"Maybe so, but it's extremely worrying that Miss Frankland-Russell has been attacked, either way. I'm just glad she managed to escape and that she seems to be recovering well."

"How do you know she's recovering well?"

"I visited her in hospital yesterday evening with Detective Inspector Fisher from Scotland Yard."

"You visited her last night? And you still didn't have the courtesy to tell me?"

"I'm sorry, Mr Bewick. I really do apologise. It's just that I've become rather embroiled in this case."

"So it seems, Mrs Peel, but you were paid to locate Miss Frankland-Russell for her family's sake. Granted, you may have found her, but you didn't keep me informed of her whereabouts. I'm sorry to have to say this, but Lord Frankland-Russell may refuse to pay you when he finds out."

"All I can do is apologise, Mr Bewick. Miss Frankland-Russell was adamant that she didn't want her parents to know where she was and, as a woman of twenty-one, she's entitled to live her life the way she sees fit. But as you've said, it's good that her parents know she's safe and well."

"And now they're extremely concerned, given that she's in hospital and they're too unwell to travel! She may be twenty-one, but that doesn't mean she knows what's best for herself. If you'd told me you had found her at the time, she could have been reunited with her parents and out of danger by now!"

The lawyer had a point, although Augusta wasn't sure the young woman could ever have been convinced to return home. She hadn't even managed to send her parents a letter.

"You mentioned an inspector from the Yard earlier," said the lawyer. "Is he investigating the terrible attack on Miss Frankland-Russell?"

"Yes. I've been assisting Detective Inspector Fisher with the investigation into two recent murders. I discovered that the victims, Elizabeth Thackeray and Dorothy Cooper, were at school with Miss Frankland-Russell. All three were involved in a tragic incident, during which a teacher died. Two other girls were also present, one of whom has since died in questionable circumstances. We don't know where the fifth young woman is at the moment, but there's a theory that the girls were attacked as an act of revenge for their involvement in the death of the teacher. That obviously can't be proven yet, but they were all very secretive when I spoke to each of them individually about their past. It all made sense once I discovered what had happened at the school."

"You think the attack on Miss Frankland-Russell may be linked to the murders of her two friends?"

"It's a strong possibility."

"And you believe the attacker intended to kill her last night?"

"Yes, I believe so."

"Well, that's very shocking indeed. I wasn't aware that there had been such a tragic incident in Miss Frankland-Russell's history."

"It's very likely that she's still in danger."

"I wouldn't be surprised from the sound of things. She needs to be kept safe until the police catch this lunatic. The best option would be to arrange for her to return to her parents' place. I shall speak to Lord Frankland-Russell first thing in the morning, and I'll also head over to the hospital to pay Miss Frankland-Russell a visit."

"She's in a quite bit of pain at the moment and is still suffering from shock, but the medical staff hope she'll make a full recovery."

"Let's hope she will. We certainly don't want to risk anything else happening to her. I shall make the necessary arrangements and do all I can to ensure that she's kept safe."

Augusta replaced the receiver on the telephone.

"Thankfully, he didn't seem to be angry with me, Sparky," she said. "I think he was more concerned about keeping Miss Frankland-Russell safe."

The telephone rang again, startling her.

This time it was Philip. "Sorry to bother you so late in the evening, Augusta."

"Oh, don't worry about that. I'd much rather speak to you than Thomas Bewick."

"Have you just been speaking to the fellow?"

"Yes and, just as you predicted, he wasn't particularly impressed with me for keeping Miss Frankland-Russell's whereabouts from him."

"Oh dear. Was he angry?"

"Not particularly, but it's unlikely that I'll be paid for my time now. Not altogether surprising, I suppose. The good news is, he's going to arrange for Miss Frankland-Russell to return home. Hopefully she'll be safe from her attacker there."

"That is good news. I'm still hoping to obtain an honest account from her about what happened to Mrs McCall, but I can only really do so once we've caught the attacker. On that note, we found something rather interesting at the Mitchells' home. How would you like to act as scribe in another interview with Walter Mitchell tomorrow? He's down at Marylebone Lane police station again. Only this time he's been arrested."

Chapter 36

"I have never laid eyes on these items before in my life," insisted Walter Mitchell the following morning.

Augusta was sitting in the interview room at Marylebone Lane police station alongside Philip and Inspector Shellbrook.

The items Walter was referring to lay on the table: a tweed overcoat, a scruffy bowler hat and a short length of thick twine.

"You say that you don't recognise these items," said Inspector Shellbrook. "But how do you explain them being found inside a sack in your backyard by a member of your house staff?"

"I really don't know!" Walter spread his hands wide. "I have no idea how they got there!" The art teacher looked even more tired than he had the previous day and he still hadn't shaved, so the stubble on his chin was quite thick.

Augusta stared at the piece of twine and felt a cold sensation in the pit of her stomach as she imagined it being used to end the lives of two young women. She shuddered and diverted her gaze.

"These items have been closely examined," said Inspector Shellbrook, "and we found a couple of straight, dark hairs on the sleeve of the jacket that appear to match Miss Frankland-Russell's hair."

Walter shrugged. "I don't doubt that, but it wasn't me!"

"Then how do you explain the twine? We know that a piece of twine or rope was used in all three attacks."

"I really cannot explain it, Inspector!

"Who else could these items possibly belong to?" asked Philip. "Your wife?"

"They don't belong to her either; not that I know of. Are you suggesting she dressed up in a man's overcoat and hat in order to attack those young women?"

"Do you think that's what happened?"

"I honestly don't know what to believe, Inspector, but I can't even begin to explain how these things were found in my backyard. Someone must have put them there."

"Yes, *someone* clearly did. The only access to your backyard is through your house, is that correct?"

"Yes, that's correct."

"So the person who put the items there must have walked through your house."

"Yes. Have you interviewed the servants yet?"

"We're in the process of doing so, and a statement has been taken from the maid who found the sack. She hadn't given it much thought until she showed it to your wife, who alerted us. We can't rule any of the servants out just yet but I'm sure you'll agree, Mr Mitchell, that you seem rather more suspicious, given that you knew Elizabeth Thackeray well and also visited Dorothy Cooper shortly before her death. And the latest victim, Catherine Frankland-Russell, works at your wife's shop. A little too much of a coincidence, I should say."

"But I was nowhere near Great Portland Street the other night!"

"You have an alibi, do you?" asked Inspector Shellbrook.

"Yes! I was at the pub."

"Which pub?"

"The Orange Tree on Euston Road."

"Is that the one close to Euston station?"

"Yes."

"That's not terribly far from Great Portland Street. How far would you say it was, Detective Inspector Fisher?"

"About half a mile."

"Not far at all. And only one stop away on the tube, too. You could have got there and back quite quickly."

"I haven't done anything wrong!" protested Walter. "This is the third time you've interviewed me. It's harassment!"

"We have very good reason to interview you again," suggested Philip.

"I'm innocent, that's all I can say on the matter. What more do you want from me?"

"Have you ever heard of Saint Mildred's school, Mr Mitchell?"

"No, where's that?"

"It's in South Hampstead."

"No."

"Did you ever know a lady named Anne McCall?"

"No, who's she?"

"She was a teacher at the school."

Mr Mitchell scratched his head. "I don't understand what all this has to do with anything, Inspector."

"Are you sure?"

Augusta watched Walter closely as he examined the grain in the tabletop. He appeared to be deep in thought.

Is he about to confess?

"We haven't got all day, Mr Mitchell," said Inspector Shellbrook. "If you've something to say, just spit it out."

"Elizabeth told me a secret once," he began, still looking down at the table. "A horrible story! It was something she'd had to live with and she made me swear never to tell anyone. I've kept it quiet for as long as I can but I suppose I should probably mention it. After all, Elizabeth's gone. There's no bringing her back now, is there?"

He lifted his eyes and addressed Philip directly. "It was when you mentioned the school just now. And the teacher. I don't know why you asked it, but Elizabeth told me about a teacher who had died, and she said that she was there at the time. She didn't tell me the name of the school or the teacher, but she told me she had nightmares about it."

"This is very interesting, Mr Mitchell. Can you tell us anything more?"

"She was with her friends. One of them was Dorothy Cooper, but I can't remember the names of the others. I only remember Dorothy because she visited her recently. Elizabeth told me that there was an argument with a teacher and that Dorothy pushed her down a flight of stairs! Unfortunately, the teacher died and the police got involved. They were all terrified that they would end up in prison! They had to pretend it was an accident, so they told the police the teacher had slipped and fallen. She wasn't a nice teacher, apparently, but I still don't think she deserved to die like that. The friends agreed that they would all cover up the truth."

"Is that why no one was willing to admit that Dorothy Cooper was responsible for the teacher's death?"

"Elizabeth said they were all close friends but they were a bit scared of Dorothy. She threatened to get them into trouble if they breathed a word of it to anyone."

"Susan Peterson and Mary Colbourne," said Philip matter-of-factly. "Who are they?"

"I don't know."

"Elizabeth never mentioned their names to you?"

"No."

"And you've never come across them yourself?"

"No."

Philip consulted his notes. "My men carried out some research, which revealed that Mary Colbourne died after falling into the River Thames in the summer of 1918. Do you know anything about that?"

"No. Why would I?"

"And Susan Peterson died the year before Miss Colbourne. Her body was also found in the river."

"Were they friends of Elizabeth's?"

"Yes. And although their deaths were treated as accidental drownings at the time, we now feel fairly sure that they were murdered."

Walter shook his head. "How dreadful," he said. "But you must understand, Inspector, that I had nothing to do with any of it."

"What do you think?" Philip asked Augusta as they left Marylebone Lane police station. "Do you think Walter Mitchell is being truthful with us?"

"He seems to be. I got the sense that he really hadn't seen those items before. It was interesting to hear that Mrs Cooper was the one who pushed Anne McCall."

"Yes, that was very interesting. I'll need to verify his account with Miss Frankland-Russell. She left the hospital last night, apparently, and is now at home with a lady constable from the Women's Police Patrol who has been tasked with keeping an eye on her."

"That's good news. Let's hope she's feeling much better by now. It's difficult to imagine why Walter Mitchell would be the murderer. He claimed not to have known the school or the teacher, so why would he seek revenge for Mrs McCall's death?"

"He could be bluffing. Maybe he does have some sort of connection to the school or Anne McCall. And don't forget that the clothing and weapon that appear to have been used in the attacks were found in his backyard."

"But why put them there? It's the sort of thing the guilty person would do if he or she deliberately wanted someone to find them. I think the sack was planted there."

"By Ellen Mitchell, perhaps?"

"Could be."

"But she called the police when the maid found the sack."

"A double bluff on her part, perhaps. Maybe she's so keen to incriminate her husband that she decided to frame him for murder. She wants to divorce him, but framing him for murder would also be a good way to get rid of him."

"What a thought! I suppose the only way to find out is to pay her another visit."

Chapter 37

ELLEN MITCHELL ROLLED her eyes as Augusta and Philip stepped inside her shop on Oxford Street. She looked as fashionable as ever in a smart lilac dress and matching headband.

"What can you possibly want with me now? Isn't it bad enough that my husband has been arrested?"

"Yes, that is rather unfortunate," replied Philip, "but it's also rather unfortunate that two girls have been murdered and a member of your staff has been attacked. I'm just as keen as you are to resolve this matter, Mrs Mitchell. Is there somewhere private we can go to talk?"

She led them into the office at the back of the shop. "If you're about to accuse me of lying again..."

"Please just allow me to ask you a few questions, Mrs Mitchell," said Philip. "We want to make this as succinct as possible. As you well know, a sack containing several suspicious items was found in the yard of your home yesterday. Have you any idea how it might have ended up there?"

She sighed. "No idea at all. I've had to reach the very unpleasant conclusion that my husband must have put it there. I can't tell you how difficult it was for me to have to consider that he may actually be guilty of such a heinous act."

"We've just spoken to him, and he denies any responsibility for the attacks."

"I suppose he would, though, wouldn't he?"

"Do you truly believe that he carried them out?"

"I honestly don't know what to think any more, Inspector."

"At the moment, Mrs Mitchell, I'm rather inclined to believe him," said Philip. "I don't think he has any idea at all how those items found their way into your backyard."

Ellen wrinkled her nose. "Really? You believe he's telling the truth?"

"Yes, I do."

She gave a sigh. "I see what you're getting at now. You think I must have had something to do with it."

"Did you?"

"No! From what I understand, the bag contained a man's overcoat, a man's hat and a piece of rope that was almost certainly used in the attacks. What would I want with a man's coat and hat? If you're suggesting that I dressed up in them and went about murdering those girls, you're quite mistaken. Inspector. I would have looked very foolish in that sort of get-up!"

"The attacks were carried out under the cover of darkness," Philip replied. "Someone who saw a dark figure wearing a long coat and hat like the ones you found might well have assumed they had seen a man, yet it's quite possible that a woman was wearing them."

"The idea seems perfectly preposterous! If it wasn't my husband, it has to have been one of the servants. Have you interviewed them yet?"

"We shall be interviewing everyone in your household,

Mrs Mitchell. You don't seem to have shown a great deal of concern for the young woman who worked for you, Catherine Frankland-Russell."

"Of course I'm concerned! It's absolutely awful that the poor girl was attacked. I still don't understand why she lied to me about who she was, though."

"She had her reasons."

"I'm sure she did! But I must say that I felt a little affronted by it. It's not right!"

"Have you visited her since the attack?"

"Not yet."

"Perhaps you should. I heard she's just returned home to continue her recovery. While we're here, have you ever heard of Saint Mildred's School, Mrs Mitchell?"

"I think so. It's in north London somewhere, isn't it?"

"Yes, South Hampstead. Have you ever been acquainted with a woman named Anne McCall?"

"No. Who's she?"

"She was a teacher at the school, but she died six years ago. I was just interested to know whether you recalled encountering her at any time."

"No. I've never visited the school, and I'm certainly not familiar with any of the teachers' names. Why are you asking me all this?"

"We're simply trying to get to the bottom of this case, Mrs Mitchell. Thank you for your time. We shall have to go and continue our investigations elsewhere."

"Do you intend to let him go?"

"Your husband, you mean?"

"Yes."

"I'll discuss it with D Division, but it's possible that we'll need to hold him until we can be quite certain that he wasn't behind the attacks."

. . .

"Do you think she was trying to frame her husband?" Augusta asked Philip as they left the shop.

"It's possible. But if she was, it would suggest that she's the one behind the murders. I can see a clear motive for her murdering Elizabeth Thackeray and, although I'm not sure what her motive would have been for attacking Catherine Frankland-Russell, there is a connection there. As for Dorothy Cooper, I've no idea why she might have wanted to murder her."

"Unless there's a connection between Ellen Mitchell and the school after all."

"Perhaps there is. That's something we'll need to find out… and soon." Philip checked his watch. "In the meantime, shall we pay Miss Frankland-Russell a quick visit? Having heard what Walter Mitchell had to say about the death of Mrs McCall, I'd like to see whether Catherine feels she can finally tell us the truth about what happened at St Mildred's."

Chapter 38

"Yeah, she's 'ere," said Catherine's red-faced landlady. "Second floor, third door along." She pointed toward the wooden staircase. "You'll see the lady constable up there."

As she climbed the creaking stairs ahead of Philip, Augusta surveyed the crumbling plasterwork and considered how different this place must be compared with the large homes Catherine Frankland-Russell had previously lived in with her family.

The police officer was sitting on a chair outside Catherine's door and she stood to her feet as they approached. Her dark blue coat was tightly belted at the waist. Her skirt was long, and she wore a wide-brimmed hat and shiny black boots.

Philip introduced himself and Augusta.

"I'm WPC Hawkins," she replied. "Miss Frankland-Russell returned home yesterday evening and my colleagues and I have been taking it in turns to keep watch here. I'm happy to say there's been nothing untoward to report at all."

"That's very good news," replied Philip. "Thank you for keeping a close eye on her."

Catherine answered the door wearing a simple brown dress and a scarf around her neck which Augusta guessed had been chosen to cover the bruising on her neck.

She gave them a weak smile as she invited them inside. "There isn't much space," she said. "I don't often have visitors here."

The room had a small kitchenette at one end and a bed and wardrobe at the other. A table with two chairs had been set up by the window. The room seemed rather bare, and Augusta realised that most of the girl's belongings were most likely inside the open trunk resting on her bed.

Catherine noticed Augusta glancing at it. "I'm returning home to my parents' house tomorrow," she said sadly. "It's probably for the best. I don't want to stay in London any longer. I need to get away."

"That sounds like a good idea," replied Augusta. "Have you spoken to them?"

"Not yet, but Mr Bewick has. He's already made the travel arrangements and he's going to accompany me there tomorrow."

"That sounds like an excellent plan," said Philip. "It's a very good idea to make peace with your parents."

"They told Mr Bewick they won't insist on me marrying Mr Farrell." She smiled. "So that's something to be pleased about."

"It certainly is!" responded Augusta, happy to hear this news. "I do hope you can be fully reconciled with them."

"Before you go," said Philip, "I'd like to hear exactly what happened during the altercation with Mrs McCall at St Mildred's."

"Oh no. Not this again!" Catherine wrapped her scarf tighter around her neck and then turned away.

"We've already heard Elizabeth Thackeray's account."

Catherine turned back to Philip. "How is that possible?"

"She told someone before she died. And that person told us."

"But we weren't ever supposed to speak of it!"

"That was an agreement you made when you were schoolgirls, isn't that right?" said Augusta. "I can quite understand why you made such an agreement back then. I'm not saying it was the right thing to do but I understand why you did it. However, that was six years ago now and Elizabeth obviously felt the need to tell someone. It was obviously too much of a burden for her to bear alone."

Catherine wiped her eyes. "It is. I try not to think about it. I've tried so hard to push it out of my mind."

"Can you tell us who pushed Mrs McCall?"

"If you've heard Elizabeth's story, you must already know."

"I'd like to hear it from you, Miss Frankland-Russell."

She shrugged. "Very well. I'm surprised she spoke about it, but I can only imagine that it was weighing too heavily on her conscience. It was Elizabeth who pushed Mrs McCall."

"Elizabeth?" queried Philip. "She said that it was Dorothy Cooper… or Dorothy Henderson, as she was then."

Catherine shook her head. "No, it was definitely Elizabeth. She clearly chose to keep lying about it right until the end."

Augusta felt astonished by this news. It seemed as though Elizabeth had wanted to confess but couldn't quite bring herself to do so. Instead, she had blamed someone else. "Why did you feel unable to tell anyone the truth until now?" she asked Catherine.

"We swore to each other that we wouldn't say anything. It was awful that Mrs McCall died, but she was so horrible to us. Cruel, even. And Mrs Jones refused to listen."

"Was Mrs Jones the headmistress at the time?"

"Yes. No one ever intended to hurt Mrs McCall, but Elizabeth just... She had a temper, and sometimes she couldn't help herself. It cast such a horrible shadow over our lives. And now Elizabeth and Dorothy are dead! Mary died years ago, too. And then he almost got me..." Catherine's hands instinctively rose to her neck, as if she were recalling the attack.

"Who might have wanted to seek revenge?" Augusta asked. "Did Mrs Mitchell have any connection to the school?"

"My manager at Stanhope Fashions? No, I don't think so."

"What about her husband?"

"Not that I know of."

"Do you believe that you were attacked as an act of revenge for Mrs McCall's death?"

"Yes, I believe I was. And I think that's why the others were attacked, too. Perhaps it's what we all deserved."

"You didn't deserve this," said Augusta. "It's not proper justice."

"And you're quite adamant that it was Elizabeth who pushed Anne McCall?" queried Philip.

Catherine nodded. "I saw it with my own eyes. Elizabeth didn't think Mrs McCall would die as a result. None of us expected that. It just all got out of hand. The whole thing haunts me still. Not a day goes by when I don't think about it. If only I hadn't been there that day! My whole life would have been so different."

Augusta shook her head. "If only you'd spoken up sooner. You could have been spared all this."

"I know, but we'd made a pact, and I hoped it would eventually be forgotten about. How foolish I was to think that!"

"I do wish you well on your return home, Miss Frankland-Russell," said Philip. "What time do you leave tomorrow?"

"The train leaves at midday from Euston, so it's only a short walk from here. I'm meeting Mr Bewick at the station."

"Good luck," said Augusta. "Perhaps I can telephone you in a few days' time to find out how you're keeping?"

Catherine smiled. "I should like that."

"Who do you really think pushed Mrs McCall?" Augusta asked Philip as they stepped out onto Longford Street.

"Probably Miss Thackeray. Or perhaps it was Mrs Cooper after all. Oh, I'm not sure we'll ever be completely certain. I'm planning to visit St Mildred's in the morning to establish which of the Mitchells had a connection to the school or to Mrs McCall. Would you like to come with me?"

"Yes, I would. Hopefully Fred will be willing to mind the shop for me again."

"I should think that he's quite used to it by now!"

"Seeing as it's close by, I'd like to pay a quick visit to Great Titchfield Street before I head back there."

"The Mitchells' house?"

"Yes. I want to see if there's any other possible way into their backyard."

"I've checked. There isn't."

"I'd just like to make doubly sure myself."

Chapter 39

Miss Roberts reluctantly agreed to meet with Augusta and Philip the following morning. Her lips were pushed firmly together and her neck and shoulders were visibly tense. If Augusta hadn't been accompanied by an inspector from Scotland Yard, she suspected the headmistress would have refused to see her. Instead, Miss Roberts stared impassively at her visitors as they sat across the desk from her.

"We're fairly certain that the recent murders have something to do with the death of Anne McCall," explained Philip. "We just have a few further questions for you about that."

"It's not a topic we often discuss here."

"So I gather."

"It's bad for morale."

"I can imagine, Miss Roberts. However, we'd like to find out whether a man named Walter Mitchell has ever worked at this school. It's most likely that he taught art, if so."

The headmistress shook her head. "I don't recall the name. However, as I explained to Mrs Peel during her last visit, I haven't been here for very long. I'll go and ask my secretary to join us. She can bring in the relevant records so we can look him up among the list of previous teachers."

She left the room and returned a short while later with a stocky, fair-haired woman. They both carried heavy books, which they placed on a table at the side of the room.

"This is my secretary, Mrs Steel," said Miss Roberts. "She doesn't recall a Mr Mitchell working here at all." She turned to the secretary. "How long have you worked here, Mrs Steel?"

"About eight years."

"Eight years," repeated Miss Roberts as she turned back to Philip and Augusta. "Do you have a rough idea of the dates he might have been here?"

"I don't," replied Philip. "In fact, it's only a guess that he ever worked here at all. Perhaps the records could be checked all the same. Do they go back as far as ten years?"

"They go back almost seventy years, Inspector."

"Well, there's obviously no need to check that far back." He gave a low chuckle in an attempt to lighten the sombre mood. It had no visible effect.

"Please begin looking through the records, Mrs Steel," instructed the headmistress. "Start in 1911, so we can cover the past ten years."

"What about a Mrs Ellen Mitchell?" asked Philip.

The headmistress sighed, as though it were impertinent to add yet another name to the mix. "I don't remember her, either. Does she bear any relation to Walter Mitchell?"

"She's his wife."

"I see."

"It's possible that her name may have been recorded as

Ellen Stanhope," Philip added. "That was her maiden name."

"Very well," replied Miss Roberts. "Did you hear that, Mrs Steel? You're looking for a Walter Mitchell and an Ellen Mitchell or Stanhope. Do any of those names ring a bell at all?"

"They don't, but I'll look them up all the same."

A few minutes later, Mrs Steel confirmed that none of these names were listed among the teachers' records.

"I've gone all the way back to 1911," she said. "Do you want me to look even further back?"

"Yes, if you wouldn't mind," replied Philip.

Augusta gave this some thought, Walter Mitchell appeared to be about forty-five years old. It was possible that he had worked at the school as far back as twenty years ago.

"We'd be going back to a time when Miss Frankland-Russell and her friends were little more than babies," she said to Philip. "Does that matter?"

He stroked his chin and gave this some thought. "I don't suppose it does. What we need to prove is whether Walter or Ellen Mitchell had any connection to the school. If it turns out they did, we'll need to establish whether they had any connection to Mrs McCall. Even if the connection goes back a long way, it may still be relevant."

They waited in silence while the secretary leafed through the book.

"No, nothing," she announced.

"Thank you for all your hard work, Mrs Steel," said the headmistress. She turned to Philip. "I'm sorry we couldn't be of more help to you, Inspector."

Philip pondered for a moment. "Is it possible that Mr and Mrs Mitchell's children attend this school?"

"Do you happen to know their names?"

He pulled out his notebook and leafed through it. "Agatha and Doris," he replied once he had found the relevant page.

"I pride myself on knowing the names of all our girls, and I'm afraid we don't have an Agatha or a Doris Mitchell here."

Philip sighed and closed his book. "Oh, well. Never mind. I was just desperately trying to find some sort of connection between the Mitchells and this school."

"I can see that. May I ask why?"

"They've both played an important part in our investigation."

Miss Roberts stood to her feet. "Well, I'm sorry that we haven't been able to find a connection for you, Inspector. Is it possible that the recent murders have nothing to do with Mrs McCall's death after all?"

"Oh, but they must do! I feel sure of it."

Miss Roberts seemed keen for them to leave, so Augusta and Philip made their way toward the door. Their visit had been frustratingly unrewarding.

Augusta was struck by a sudden thought. She stopped and turned to face Miss Roberts. "Mrs McCall…" she commented.

"Yes."

"Was she married?"

"I assume so."

"She was widowed," said Mrs Steel. "Her husband died young. I recall that she came to work here shortly after his death."

"Was her maiden name Mitchell, by any chance?" asked Augusta.

"I don't know," replied the headmistress.

The secretary shrugged.

"Yes, there could be something in that idea, Augusta!"

said Philip, his eyes wide. "If her maiden name was Mitchell, she may have been related to Walter Mitchell. Or perhaps her maiden name was Stanhope. That way she may have been related to Ellen Mitchell. Who could tell us, do you think?"

"The games mistress I spoke to during my last visit!" said Augusta, her heart began to pound with excitement. "Miss Worsley. Would she know?"

"She may well do," responded the headmistress, "but she'll be teaching at the moment."

"Then interrupt her!" replied Philip. "This is very important, Miss Roberts. If Mrs McCall was related to Walter or Ellen Mitchell, we need to know as a matter of urgency!"

The headmistress walked over to the door. "If you insist, Inspector, I shall go and fetch her right away. I do hope all this will be worth our while."

The window of the office overlooked the school field. Augusta and Philip watched as the thin, grey figure of Miss Roberts strode out across the green expanse toward the games mistress, who was overseeing hockey drills.

A short while later, Miss Worsley entered the office alongside Miss Roberts, her face had been reddened by the cold wind.

"I've already asked the games mistress your question, Inspector," said Miss Roberts. "However, I can tell you now that it's not Mitchell. Or Stanhope, either, for that matter."

"That's a shame," replied Philip. "We won't keep you much longer, Miss Worsley. For what it's worth, would you mind telling us the name Mrs McCall was known by before she married?"

"I can't remember it exactly, but I know that it began with a 'b'. Berwick, I think it was."

Augusta jumped. "*Bewick?*" she asked.

"Could have been."

Philip turned to Augusta and she could see in his eyes that he had reached the same conclusion as her.

Thomas Bewick. The Frankland-Russells' solicitor.

"He's meeting her at Euston to take her home!" Augusta exclaimed.

Philip nodded. "Midday, didn't she say?"

Augusta glanced up at the clock on the mantelpiece. It was twenty-past eleven.

"I need to make a quick telephone call," said Philip. "Can I please use your telephone, Miss Roberts? I'll make sure the Yard reimburses you for the call."

"Of course. What's the significance of all this? Is it something to do with the surname Berwick?"

"Bewick," replied Philip as he picked up the receiver. Once through to the telephone exchange, he asked to be connected to Lord Frankland-Russell. "Do you happen to know where in Shropshire they live, Augusta?" he asked. "The operator wants an address."

Augusta took a deep breath, desperately trying to recall the name of the house Lady Hereford had mentioned. It was on the tip of her tongue… "Harkup!" she said finally. "Harkup House. I don't know whereabouts in Shropshire that is, though."

"Hopefully that'll be enough." He relayed this to the operator and was finally put through to the Frankland-Russell residence.

Augusta tried to accustom herself to the idea that Thomas Bewick was somehow related to Anne McCall. The shared surname was too much of a coincidence for them not to be connected. *Is he her brother?*

Philip briefly spoke to a staff member at the household before connecting with Lord Frankland-Russell. "I'm telephoning to ask whether you're expecting your daughter, Catherine, to arrive home today... She's due to leave London by train shortly... Your solicitor is accompanying her... Thomas Bewick..."

A minute later, Philip replaced the telephone receiver. "The old boy had no idea what I was talking about," he said. "He wasn't expecting Miss Frankland-Russell home today. And as for Thomas Bewick, he's never heard of the man!"

Chapter 40

"So that's why he wanted me to find her!" exclaimed Augusta.

"What's going on?" asked Miss Roberts.

"I need to make another telephone call," replied Philip, picking up the telephone receiver. He put in a call to Scotland Yard and requested assistance at Euston station. Then he rang off. "We need to get going, Augusta."

Outside, they hurried toward Finchley Road. "Bewick wanted Catherine dead," said Augusta, "but he couldn't track her down because she'd changed her name!"

They stopped outside a public house, desperately searching for a taxi. A steady stream of traffic flowed past them.

Philip checked his watch. "We've only got half an hour!"

"We have to get there before twelve," said Augusta. "Can't you just flag down another vehicle?"

"I might have to. I'd prefer to take a taxi, as the drivers know how to pick up the pace when they need to. Oh, there's one over on the other side of the road!" Philip waved his walking stick at it. "Over here!" he yelled.

The taxi eventually slowed, swung around and stopped by the kerbside.

"Euston station, as quickly as you can please," urged Philip, showing the driver his warrant card.

The driver nodded and they were off.

Augusta's mind whirled as she attempted to understand what had happened. "He tracked down the other girls," she said, "but he couldn't find Miss Frankland-Russell. And I've gone and helped him. I've delivered her right into his hands!"

"You weren't to know, Augusta. He fooled us all."

"That explains why he asked me not to contact her parents. They had no idea what he was up to! Miss Frank-land-Russell thought it odd that they would suddenly want to find her again. As far as she was concerned, they had washed their hands of her." Augusta felt a pang of anger. "And to think that I felt such sympathy for them! I felt so bad that they were missing their daughter and wanted to find out where she was. It was all lies!"

"He's certainly a master manipulator," responded Philip. "I'm concerned about what he intends to do to Miss Frankland-Russell once he gets hold of her. The best thing we can do now is hurry to Euston and stop them before they get on that train."

The taxi made its way south toward Regent's Park.

"If Thomas Bewick did murder those girls," said Philip, "he somehow managed to plant that sack of clothing in the Mitchells' yard. He knew where they lived because he was assisting Ellen Mitchell with her divorce, wasn't he? I imagine he must have visited the house at some point. But how did he leave the sack there without anyone noticing? I'm sure the servants would have mentioned something if he'd turned up at the house with it."

"I'm fairly confident he didn't," replied Augusta, recalling her recent visit to Great Titchfield Street. "I took a little walk around the area, do you remember? I couldn't see any way that the yard might be accessed from Great Titchfield Street because the buildings are terraced, so I decided to visit the street the Mitchells' house backs on to. It's called Hanson Street and the buildings are all terraced there too. There are no little lanes or alleyways that would afford anyone access to the back yards. There is, however, a public house. It wouldn't surprise me if the pub had a yard from which Bewick managed to throw the sack into the Mitchells' yard. It's just a theory, but it could explain how he was able to get it there without anyone noticing."

"Do you know for sure that the pub's yard is close enough to the Mitchells'?"

"I wasn't completely sure but we could go there and check. After we've apprehended Bewick himself, that is."

"I hope we're not too late." Philip glanced out of the window. "The traffic's building up." He knocked on the partition separating them from the driver. "Can't we get round this somehow? We need to be at Euston within twenty minutes!"

"I'm doin' me best!" responded the cab driver. He steered around the van in front of them and picked up the pace.

Philip slumped back in his seat. "If both my legs worked properly I'd just sprint through Regent's Park and be there in no time. I suppose we could always get the next train if we miss them at the station."

"But what if they don't actually get on the train? Miss Frankland-Russell told us that Mr Bewick was meeting her there to take the midday train, but maybe he's planning to whisk her away somewhere else."

"That's a good point. He can't do her much harm in the middle of a busy station but, if he persuades her to go somewhere else, who knows what could happen?"

"I don't see how he'd manage that. It would almost certainly make her suspicious."

"It's possible that they'll catch the train, but perhaps he'll persuade her to disembark early rather than taking her all the way to Shropshire."

Augusta shuddered. "She's in terrible danger and there's nothing we can do to warn her! She trusts him. We all trusted him!"

The traffic was beginning to clear a little. They passed London Zoo and the boundary of Regent's Park before turning left into a narrow street behind Euston station.

Philip checked his watch. "Only fifteen minutes to go. Come on, come on…" His foot tapped impatiently. "London's roads are so busy these days."

"Almos' there!" called out the cab driver.

Augusta gave a sigh of relief as she saw the long, pitched roofs of the station up ahead. The taxi turned left, then abruptly stopped.

"Workmen in the road!" he called out. "I'll 'ave to take you rahnd the long way."

"No need, we'll walk from here!" replied Philip.

They clambered out of the cab and quickly paid the fare, then they hurried toward the station. Still reliant on his stick, Philip could only manage a steady walk.

"You go on ahead, Augusta. See if you can find them inside the station. I'll catch you up."

"Right! I'll see you in there," she responded, jogging toward the station entrance. Once inside, she pushed her way through a throng of people gathered outside a small parade of shops. Entering the main hall, she looked about frantically for a uniformed member of staff she could ask about departures to Shropshire. The large clock in the that it was five minutes to midday. She didn't have much time.

Apologising to a long queue of people, she interrupted the traveller at the front, who was in the process of purchasing a ticket, to ask about the Shropshire departure. "I'm working on behalf of Scotland Yard!" she added to appease the grumpy-looking ticket clerk.

"Platform two," he responded.

She thanked him, then dodged her way through the crowds in the direction of the platforms. With her heart pounding and her head spinning, she searched frantically for overhead signs bearing the platform numbers.

A group of puzzled-looking constables had also arrived, presumably dispatched by the message from Scotland Yard. Augusta dashed up to them. "We're looking for a man aged about fifty with grey hair," she said. "He's always smartly dressed. He'll be with a young woman. Possibly near platform two!"

"Alright."

She didn't have time to explain any further. She went off and found platform two, then slowed her pace a little and surveyed the crowd around her. *Are they here?*

There was no sign of them.

Perhaps they're already on the train.

She ran up to it. What appeared to be the last of the luggage was being loaded into the guard's van and a number of people were saying their farewells.

Should I get on? Are they even on the train?

"Augusta!"

She turned around to see Philip approaching.

"Any sign of them?" he called out.

She shook her head. "I can't see them."

The guard's whistle blew.

Chapter 41

"THERE GOES THE GUARD'S WHISTLE," said Thomas. "Looks like we'll be leaving on time." He gave Catherine a smile that didn't reach his eyes.

She was seated opposite him in the first-class train compartment, perched stiffly on the plush velvet seat. She was struggling to relax in his company. His pale blue eyes always seemed to be on her, as though he were carefully watching her every move. Now and again, one side of his mouth lifted slightly in an expression of contempt.

He's only supposed to be escorting me to Shropshire. Why does he keep looking at me like that?

"Three and a half hours to Shrewsbury," he continued. "We should be at your parents' home by half-past four. I've telephoned ahead, and they'll be sending someone to meet us off the train."

Three and a half hours in a small compartment with this man. For some reason, she didn't feel comfortable alone with him. *I hope someone else joins us soon.*

"Your parents will be so pleased to see you," Thomas said.

"Is that what they told you?"

"Yes! They sounded overjoyed."

"I still can't understand what made them change their minds."

The smile dropped from his face surprisingly quickly. "Something must have happened to help them realise how precious you are to them. Never underestimate the importance of family, Miss Frankland-Russell."

The whistle blew again and several doors slammed shut. Catherine jumped. The sudden noises jarred her nerves. She wasn't usually like this but, ever since the attack, she had felt fearful all the time, as though something were lurking behind her waiting to strike the first moment she became distracted.

Catherine still felt bruised, too. She hoped she would be able to rest at her parents' home. *Will they leave me in peace and allow me to recuperate?* That was what she needed. She felt happy to be escaping London. All she had to do was endure the train journey and then she would be safe.

But what if the killer tracks me down to Shropshire? Catherine felt a shiver at the thought. She wouldn't be able to rest until the police caught him. *I should have known that all those years of lying wouldn't go unpunished. If only I'd told the truth from the outset, none of this would have happened. What if the police never catch him? Am I destined to spend the rest of my life looking over my shoulder?*

A middle-aged lady in a purple hat looked into the compartment as she walked along the corridor. Seeing four spare seats, she slid the door open to come in.

"I hope you don't think me rude, madam," said Mr Bewick, "but my daughter and I would prefer to travel alone."

The lady frowned, but she clearly wasn't in the mood

to argue about it. She closed the door again and walked on down the corridor.

Catherine felt a prickle at the back of her neck. *Something doesn't feel right.* "Why did you ask her to leave us alone?" she queried.

He smiled vacuously again. "I thought we could discuss your parents' affairs while we travel. They're confidential matters, of course, so I wouldn't want anybody to overhear our conversation."

That sounds like a plausible explanation. Perhaps there's no reason for me to feel jumpy after all.

Catherine rested back against the seat and tried to make herself as comfortable as possible as the train pulled out of the station.

Chapter 42

AUGUSTA AND PHILIP found themselves standing in a third-class carriage.

"They're not likely to be travelling in here, are they?" said Philip. "Having met Thomas Bewick, he strikes me as the sort who would travel first-class. We'll have to walk all the way to the front of the train."

Beyond the window, Augusta could see the platform slipping away. The train passed over a set of points before beginning to pick up speed.

Augusta and Philip walked along the corridor, passing several compartments as they went. When they reached the end of the carriage, Philip tried the handle of the door leading into the next section of the train.

"It's locked," he said.

"Now what?" replied Augusta. "Do we have to jump out at the next station to access the next carriage? It'll take us forever to get through the whole train!"

"I'll summon the guard and ask him to unlock the doors for us."

Philip stepped into the nearest passenger compartment,

apologised to its occupants, then reached up and pulled the communication cord above the window.

The train jolted and shook as it slowed to a stop.

Philip left the compartment and grimaced. "Train guards never like it when you pull the chain. He'll be angry, just you wait and see."

A moment later, the guard marched up the corridor from his van at the rear of the train. "Was that you?" he barked at Philip.

"Yes, it was." Philip showed the guard his warrant card. "I need to apprehend someone who I believe is on this train. Can you please unlock the doors between the carriages so I can find him?"

"Which carriage is he in?"

"I don't know yet. Probably first-class, but I'll need to search the entire train."

The guard sighed. "Right. Well, I'd like to get it moving again, if that's all right with you, Inspector. We're holding up all the trains travelling behind us. Are you happy for us to proceed to Watford while you look for your man?"

"More than happy," replied Philip. "Thank you."

The guard pushed open a window and blew his whistle, signalling to the driver that the train was ready to move again. Then he proceeded to unlock the door to the next carriage and walked on ahead of them.

"Let's keep looking for them," said Philip, following behind. "Although we may discover that they're not on board after all."

They walked through the next carriage, glancing into each compartment. Augusta found herself moving faster than Philip. She was beginning to doubt whether Miss Frankland-Russell and Mr Bewick were on the train after all.

"Why have we stopped?" asked Catherine. She glanced around. The train was in a cutting, with grimy brick walls rising up on either side of the railway line.

"I don't know." Thomas stood. He slid the window down and peered out, swiftly ducking his head back in as a train passed by in the opposite direction. "That was a close one," he commented. He pushed the window back up and returned to his seat. "Nothing to see out there. Perhaps some poor fellow found himself on the wrong train. No need to go pulling the emergency cord for that, though."

Thomas's foot was tapping impatiently and the noise irritated Catherine. There seemed to be something tense and restless about him. *Is he always like this?*

The tapping eased as the train began to move again. Thomas picked up his newspaper, glanced down at it, then tossed it to one side.

Is he planning to start talking about my family's confidential affairs soon? Catherine hoped he would get it over and done with quickly so she could rest. She turned to look out of the window, spotting a number of red-brick warehouses, goods sheds and a line of tall houses.

Thomas also seemed to be looking out of the window, albeit rather more intently. *Is he looking out for a particular landmark?*

Grimy walls rose up on either side of them again, the buildings perched high above them.

Mr Bewick pulled at his collar then clasped his hands together.

Something's bothering him, but what? Why can't he sit still? The situation didn't seem right at all. Catherine's mouth felt dry.

She was just about to excuse herself and take a walk

along the corridor, when the train entered a tunnel. The compartment was instantly plunged into darkness.

Catherine heard a swift movement just a split second before a hand wrapped around her neck.

"You got away from me last time," he hissed in her ear. "But you won't escape this time!"

She managed to let out a pained cry before his hand tightened around her throat. She frantically tried to pull it away, kicking out wildly with her legs, but she couldn't draw any air into her lungs.

The pressure on her neck released for a brief moment. It took her a moment to understand why. She heard the latch of the train door, then felt a sudden rush of cold air.

Does he intend to push me out?

I'll have to fight as hard as I can.

Thomas tried to get his arms around her, but she refused to let him lift her. She lashed out with her hands and managed to tug at his hair, causing him to cry out.

He hauled her up from her seat and she fell to the floor.

I have to stay down here. I can't let him push me out of the carriage.

~

Augusta cursed under her breath as the train went dark. She had just stepped into the next carriage and she couldn't see a thing. She pulled her torch out of her handbag.

Having travelled the same route before, Augusta guessed they were in the long tunnel that passed beneath Primrose Hill. As she lingered in the corridor, she heard a thud, then a stifled yelp.

Startled, she slid open the door of the compartment

closest to her. "Is there anyone in here?" she flashed the torch around and was met with silence.

Augusta made her way to the next compartment. As she slid open the door, she instantly sensed that something was wrong. Cold air rushed toward her, the carriage door was open.

A man crouched over a woman on the floor. He seemed to be pushing her toward the open door.

"Help!" The woman's face turned toward her.

Catherine Frankland-Russell.

Augusta dropped the torch as she lunged forward and grabbed hold of Thomas's arm, pulling as hard as she could.

"Get off!" he shouted, pushing her back.

Although she lacked the strength to pull him away from Miss Frankland-Russell, Augusta hoped she would be able to prevent him from pushing her out of the train. Barely able to see a thing, she prayed they would be out of the tunnel soon. She reached out again and pulled at Thomas's jacket.

"Get off her!" she yelled.

She was getting nowhere.

"Augusta?" came a shout from behind her.

It was Philip.

He helped her tug at Thomas's jacket, both desperate to stop him causing Catherine any further harm.

To Augusta's relief, the train finally left the tunnel and light flooded the carriage.

Philip hooked his hands under the lawyer's arms and hauled him to his feet. Catherine clambered up onto the seat, breathless with exertion, her eyes wide.

"Thomas Bewick, you're under arrest!" shouted Philip.

The lawyer twisted round and punched his captor on the jaw. Philip recoiled, clutching his face. Thomas leapt over to the open door and pulled the emergency chain above the window.

Augusta gripped the luggage rack above the seat as the train ground to a juddering halt.

"Stop right there!" cried Philip.

"I don't think so," panted Bewick, stepping ever closer to the open door.

"Don't you move!"

The lawyer laughed and jumped out of the carriage.

He had escaped.

"I don't believe it," puffed Philip. "He's got away."

Moments later, a train thundered past on the adjacent track.

Chapter 43

"I honestly don't mind looking after the shop again today, Mrs Peel," said Fred Plummer. "You must be exhausted after your ordeal yesterday."

"Thank you, Fred. It wasn't as much of an ordeal for me as it was for Miss Frankland-Russell, but at least she's all right. It's very kind of you to offer but I think I've deserted you enough over the past week or so. I'm sure today will be a much quieter day."

"The man who attacked her was killed by a train, wasn't he?"

Augusta winced at the memory. "Yes, he was. I suppose it means nobody has to waste any more time tracking him down. I feel terribly sorry that his sister died in such a tragic way, but taking matters into his own hands was hardly the way to solve it."

"I read all about it in this morning's newspaper," said Fred. "He'd obviously decided to carry out his own form of justice."

"He was fairly successful in his own warped way. That's how those four poor girls lost their lives. It's terribly sad. At least he can't cause any more harm now."

The bell above the door sounded as Philip walked in. "Morning, Augusta, Fred. I don't have long, I'm afraid, I need to finish writing up my report for the commissioner. I just wanted to stop by to see how you were this morning, Augusta."

"I'm well, thank you. And very relieved that the case has finally been brought an end."

"I've discovered that Bewick went to great lengths to cover his tracks. I spoke to his secretary yesterday evening and, can you believe, he even went to the trouble of hand-writing letters to Lord Frankland-Russell? She typed the letters for him but they were never posted. He was very keen to keep up the pretence that he was working for the family; even his secretary was taken in."

"How is Catherine?"

"She was still keen to return to her parents yesterday evening, so I telephoned them again and explained what had happened. They were extremely shocked, as you'd expect. But they sounded eager to see their daughter again, having learned of the danger she'd found herself in. I believe she's planning to travel up there today."

"If only the St Mildred's girls had been honest with the police from the outset."

"Only one was responsible but the others were too scared to say anything. They were young, I suppose, and they all felt a sense of loyalty toward their friend."

"Anne McCall died six years ago. Why do you think Mr Bewick waited until now to avenge her?"

"He didn't wait as long as it might seem. Susan Peterson died in 1917, and Mary Colbourne passed away the following year. For some reason, it took him a couple of years longer to find the others."

"All apart from Miss Frankland-Russell. He needed my help with that." Augusta shook her head again, still dismayed that she had been fooled by him.

"At least Walter Mitchell will get a break from me now," said Philip with a laugh. "I wonder if his wife will push for the divorce."

"She'll have to find herself a new lawyer if she decides to go ahead."

They were distracted by a movement just beyond the shop window.

"Well I never," commented Philip. "It's Lady Hereford!"

He stepped forward to open the door and in came the old lady, wrapped in a thick fur coat and being pushed along in a wicker bath chair by a maid.

"Oh, look at this place, Augusta!" she exclaimed. "What a cosy little bookshop!" she glanced up at them all. "And who's this handsome young man?"

"My new sales assistant, Fred Plummer."

"Nice to meet you, Fred. How lovely that you have some help now, Augusta. You have a terrible habit of trying to do everything all by yourself. And the dashing Detective Inspector Fisher is here, too. How are you, sir?"

"Less of the dashing, Lady Hereford. I'm rather tired, if truth be told."

"I read all about that train drama in this morning's newspaper. The news reporter interviewed you, did he not?"

"Yes, that's the problem these days. News reporters won't leave you alone until they've got every last drop of information out of you. Hopefully everything will quieten down now and Miss Frankland-Russell will be able to lead a nice quiet life up in Shropshire.

"Indeed. Oh, I spy my little Sparky! Wheel me over to him please," she instructed the maid.

The old lady opened the cage door and gave a low whistle. The canary returned it in song.

"It's so lovely to see you again, Sparky. How I've missed you!"

"He's missed you, too, Lady Hereford," said Augusta.

"Don't be silly! He hasn't missed me a jot. I can tell that he's perfectly happy here. He's probably forgotten all about me!" She turned to the canary. "Now, the question is, Sparky, do you want to come and live with me again? Or would you prefer to stay here with Mrs Peel?"

The End

Historical Note

Bloomsbury is an area of central London with a rich cultural and educational heritage. The area was first laid out in the eighteenth century and gradually developed around ten formal squares landscaped with lawns and trees. Much of the development provided large, attractive homes for wealthy families. Bomb damage during the Second World War and subsequent rebuilding changed the character of some of the squares, Bedford Square remains the best preserved.

The area has long been associated with literary figures, Charles Dickens lived in Bloomsbury once he'd found success and the 'Bloomsbury Set' - a group of writers, thinkers and artists - were based here in the early twentieth century. Notable members were Virginia Woolf, John Maynard Keynes, Lytton Strachey and EM Forster. Other famous Bloomsbury residents have included Dorothy L Sayers, JM Barrie, Vladimir Lenin and Christina Rossetti.

The British Museum is located in Bloomsbury as are the headquarters of the University of London and three of its colleges: University College London, Birkbeck College and the School of Oriental and African Studies.

The Slade School of Fine Art is an art college at University College London. It was founded in 1868 and has an impressive list of alumni, the artist Lucian Freud was a tutor at the school from 1949-54.

Paddington Street Gardens was originally a burial ground for St Marylebone parish church. After being closed to burials in the early nineteenth century, the area opened as a public recreation ground in 1885. Apparently some of the original lime and London plane trees planted at this time are still standing.

The WPC looking after Catherine Frankland-Russell is a member of the Metropolitan Police Women Patrols. The first female police officers were in the Women Police Volunteers, an organisation founded in 1914 by suffragettes Nina Boyle and Margaret Damer Dawson. The founding of the organisation was in response to the dwindling number of male police officers (as men were called up to fight in the First World War) as well as concern for the number of female refugees who were arriving in London alone and at risk of exploitation. Also at this time, Scotland Yard approached the National Union of Women Workers to set up women patrols in London.

The Metropolitan Police Women Patrols came into service on 17th February 1919. The first three sergeants were Grace Russell, Patty Alliot and Lilian Wyles. Recruits had to be aged between 25 and 38 and taller than 5'4". They had no power of arrest.

Female police officers worked in separate units to their male colleagues until the 1970s when the Equal Pay Act and Sexual Discrimination Act led to full integration.

The tunnel which the train enters in the closing chapters of the book is Primrose Hill Tunnel in north west London, about two miles from Euston station. It's over a kilometre long and was the first railway tunnel in London. It took four years to construct, from 1833 - 1837. Construction was difficult because it proved a challenge trying to bore through the London clay. There was public unease about travelling on a train through a long tunnel so, before it opened, four doctors were consulted on the "effect of such a tunnel on the health and feelings". They concluded that travelling in a train through the tunnel would be no different to travelling in a coach along a narrow street at night.

Thank you

∼

Thank you for reading *The Bloomsbury Murder* I really hope you enjoyed it!

Would you like to know when I release new books? Here are some ways to stay updated:

- Like my Facebook page:
  facebook.com/emilyorganwriter
- Follow me on Goodreads:
  goodreads.com/emily_organ
- Follow me on BookBub: bookbub.com/authors/emily-organ
- View my other books here: emilyorgan.com

Thank you

And if you have a moment, I would be very grateful if you would leave a quick review of *The Bloomsbury Murder* online. Honest reviews of my books help other readers discover them too!

The Penny Green Series

Also by Emily Organ. Escape to 1880s London! A page-turning historical mystery series.

As one of the first female reporters on 1880s Fleet Street, plucky Penny Green has her work cut out. Whether it's investigating the mysterious death of a friend or reporting on a serial killer in the slums, Penny must rely on her wits and determination to discover the truth.

Fortunately she can rely on the help of Inspector James Blakely of Scotland Yard, but will their relationship remain professional?

Find out more here: emilyorgan.com/penny-green-victorian-mystery-series

The Churchill & Pemberley
Series

Also by Emily Organ. Join senior sleuths Churchill and Pemberley as they tackle cake and crime in an English village.

Growing bored in the autumn of her years, Londoner Annabel Churchill buys a private detective agency in a Dorset village. The purchase brings with it the eccentric Doris Pemberley and the two ladies are soon solving mysteries and chasing down miscreants in sleepy Compton Poppleford.

Plenty of characters are out to scupper their chances, among them grumpy Inspector Mappin. Another challenge is their four-legged friend who means well but has a problem with discipline.

But the biggest challenge is one which threatens to derail every case they work on: will there be enough tea and cake?

Find out more here: emilyorgan.com/the-churchill-pemberley-cozy-mystery-series

Made in United States
Troutdale, OR
07/07/2023